# FROM THE HORSE'S MOUTH

ALSO BY KATHY MACKEL

CAN OF WORMS

EGGS IN ONE BASKET

# FROM THE HORSE'S MOUTH

## KATHY MACKEL

HarperCollins*Publishers*

From the Horse's Mouth
Copyright © 2002 by Kathy Mackel
HarperCollins Children's Books, a division of HarperCollins
Publishers, 1350 Avenue of the Americas, New York, NY 10019.
www.harperchildrens.com

Library of Congress Cataloging-in-Publication Data
Mackel, Kathy.
  From the horse's mouth / Kathy Mackel.
    p.   cm.
  Sequel to: Eggs in one basket.
  Summary: Smart-aleck middle-school student Nick Thorpe and
popular high school princess Jill Pillsbury battle villains from
outer space in an attempt to save the glorious time-warping
Zephyr.
  ISBN 0-06-029414-0 — ISBN 0-06-029415-9 (lib. bdg.)
  [1. Extraterrestrial beings—Fiction. 2. Schools—Fiction.
3. Science fiction.]  I. Title.
PZ7.M1955 Fr  2002                              2001039819
[Fic]—dc21                                            CIP
                                                       AC

          1  2  3  4  5  6  7  8  9  10
                       ❖
                  First Edition

TO DAN AND JAMIE,
ON THE GLITTERING PATH

## ACKNOWLEDGMENTS

Special thanks to my husband, Steve, who lets me get away with more than I deserve, and to my writers group—Kate Berquist, Dave Daniel, Judy Loose, Bev McCoy, Chuck Osberg, Marj Overhiser, Kristi Perko, Bob Sanchez, Patty Thorpe, and Dave Tuells—who don't let me get away with anything.

FROM THE
HORSE'S MOUTH

# 1

**iF ONLY i HAD KEPT MY MOUTH SHUT.**

That's going to be on my tombstone: *Here lies Nicholas Thorpe. He would have lived a long life . . . if only he had kept his mouth shut.*

It was all Fleming's fault. If he had kept *his* mouth shut, I would have been on my way to fourth-block science instead of the twilight zone.

But when Fleming flashed me that gap where his two front teeth used to be, that black hole that made him look like a kindergartner with zits and face fuzz—well, I just had to say something.

"What happened to you, Fleming? Floss with a chain saw?"

"You know what happened to me, jerk." Fleming's front teeth had been knocked out in a football game. His parents' insurance hadn't come through yet with the money to buy him new ones, so he walked around spitting through a hole big enough for a dump truck to drive through.

I dreaded the day Fleming came into Ashby Middle School with a new toothpaste smile and ruined all my fun. Until then, I had a ready-made target.

"What's that?" I said, pretending to be hard of hearing. "You got it from kissing too hard? That'll teach you to practice on your vacuum cleaner." Laughter erupted—my fellow seventh graders were eating out of my hand. And that was, of course, the point of this whole exercise.

The warning bell rang. The kids shuffled their books, ready to head off to class. Time to end another flawless Nick Thorpe roast. But when Fleming yelled "Take it back, you thlimeball," my fate was sealed.

"*Th*limeball?" I snorted. "Watch it! You're spitting—I mean, *th*pitting *th*aliva all over the*the* poor kid*th*!"

My fans held their books over their heads, fending off Fleming's imaginary spit storm.

Fleming glared. "Thee what you thtarted? Thut up, Thorpe!"

"Or what?" I made a dramatic show of wiping spit out of my eye. "You gonna beat the *th*not out of me?"

Fleming hoisted me against the wall. A hundred and eighty pounds of dumb muscle drew a bead on

**2**

my face. My heart pounded in my throat, so loud that the *thum-thum-thum* seemed to be coming from outside me. *Now would be a good time to take it back*, I told myself.

But when Fleming roared, "I'm gonna thmack you into tomorrow!" I laughed. I was still laughing when Fleming's fist came crashing toward my nose.

Still laughing as I tumbled toward tomorrow.

*I'm dead*, I thought as I disappeared in a bright flash.

*I'm alive*, I thought as I bounced hard onto the floor.

*I'm alive and in heaven*, I thought as I swam in a sea of long legs, perfect teeth, and clear skin.

Aaron Fleming had knocked me clear across the school, into an all-girl aerobics class.

"Good morning, ladies!" I said with my best talk show–host smile.

The workout room was dead silent. It was an unbelievable moment—ten females and not one was talking. Even stranger, there was no pounding of feet, no grinding of the overhead fans, no blasting from the CD player.

Had I shocked them into silence? "Hey, anyone still on this planet?" I yelled.

Each girl was frozen in mid-motion, as if someone had hit the pause button on a VCR. A freckle-faced girl with blazing red hair stood with her leg pointed high in the air. A girl with spiky blond hair and fat cheeks grinned like a circus clown.

"Good joke! Mega ha-ha's and all that." I chuckled. "You can resume living now."

No one moved. Not a hair, not a whisper. I tapped the red-haired girl on the shoulder. "Hey. Twinkle Toes. What's happening?"

My hand went *through* her shoulder.

I stumbled back, knocking into the spike-haired girl. Except I passed right through her, too, and bounced off the back wall.

I freaked, jumping and shouting and racing around. But it was like running through a room of ghosts—no one moved, no one spoke, no one breathed.

*Chill, Thorpe*, I warned myself. *Cardiac arrest at the age of thirteen just ain't cool.* I forced a deep breath, then another. *Exhale. Focus!*

The clock on the wall read 12:05. My watch read 10:44. The seconds ticked along on my wrist while the hands on the wall clock sat still. My throat tightened, and I choked back puke.

Heaven had become aerobics class. And now aerobics class had become the twilight zone. Or worse. Maybe I had just mouthed off one too many times. Maybe Fleming really did kill me.

Maybe I was condemned to an eternity of detention.

☆   ☆   ☆

4

The door to the hall was held open by a girl in a red T-shirt. A bead of sweat dripped down her cheek. Except it didn't drip—it just hung there. "Hey, you're leaking," I joked.

She didn't laugh with me.

I stepped around her, into the hall.

And bumped *through* my science teacher, Mr. Fitz-Patrick. "Well, excuse the heck out of me, Mr. FitzPatrick."

Nothing. The hair in his nose pushed outward and I realized he had been caught exhaling.

I stepped around him and continued on down the hall. It was the same old Ashby Middle School—classrooms in the proper places, holes in the right walls, posters hung on the correct doors.

But nothing moved. So weird.

That's what is going to be on Mike Pillsbury's tombstone: *Here lies Albert Michael Pillsbury . . . he raised Weird to an art form.*

If anyone could explain this twilight zone, my best friend and master of the universe, Mike Pillsbury, could.

# 2

I FOUND MIKE IN THE SECOND-FLOOR boys' lavatory, flossing his teeth.

He was frozen mid-swipe, his tongue sticking out like a pink slug. A hunk of snot hung off the dental floss. I gagged, then realized the green clump was broccoli.

Vegetarian pizza was on the lunch menu that day. Even though my watch now read 11:18, Mike was fishing the last bite of lunch from between his teeth. Seventh graders had lunch from 11:35 to 12:10. Mike usually slipped to the bathroom for the last five minutes to do tooth patrol. The clock in the workout room had read 12:05, so, as illogical as this world was, it was logical that Mike should be here.

That nosewipe Fleming had threatened to punch

me into tomorrow. But he had only succeeded in getting me to lunchtime.

So where was Nick Thorpe in all this? Was I already here, a statue like everyone else? Or was I just in this weird la-la land, waiting to get here? And would I ever get here—or there—or back to where I was—or forward to where I should be?

My brain was ready to burst.

Leaving Mike to meditate on his molars, I dashed downstairs to the cafeteria. The swinging doors were closed, and, though they were solid in my hand, I couldn't budge them. Apparently in this weird world, if a door was closed I couldn't open it and if it was open I couldn't close it. Everything had to remain as it was.

I climbed the trophy case that proudly displayed Ashby Middle School's triumphs in the hall outside the lunchroom. I peered through the upper windows into the cafeteria. Most of the seventh grade was still in there; everyone except me.

The top of the trophy case was covered with a decade of dust, but I hadn't disturbed one speck. Where I had yanked myself up, where I had knelt, even where I had turned around, the dust still lay in a heavy coating, as if I had never been there.

But if I wasn't in the lunchroom and wasn't where I thought I had just been, where was I?

What if I wasn't anywhere?

I decided if I was going to live forever in this freak show, I'd at least find something good to look at.

The girls' locker room had a changing area with rows of mesh lockers, a shower room to the right, and the lavatory to the left. Over the partial wall that separated the showers from the lockers, I could see water frozen, mid-spray, from a row of showers.

It would be just a matter of peeking around the curtains.

Then my gut turned sour. "What're you doing, fool?" I said aloud. I was the master of the cheap shot, but this was too cheap, even for me.

Spying on girls in the locker room would be a record achievement. But if I were to do this now, while the girls were defenseless, I'd be a bigger scum than the mildew crawling up the tiles.

I walked out of the shower room, half of me feeling like a hero, the other half feeling like a sucker.

A hum rose around me, distant but strong, like a plane flying just over the horizon. My stomach dropped—after two hours of complete silence, the sound scared the heck out of me.

The air waved and danced, like a breeze over hot pavement on a summer day. Colors jumped in front of me. An outline of a person took form . . . with a sick feeling deep in my gut, I looked at myself. "What are you doing here?" I whispered.

My question was drowned out by a shout as the girls came to life in a fit of screaming. A roar swept over me as I tumbled back into *now*.

And into a whole mess of trouble.

# 3

BY THE TIME PRINCIPAL GOODRICH finished with me, I had a five-day in-house suspension. My mother, Alice Thorpe, was not amused. "Another suspension? If your father was here . . ."

"But my father isn't here," I snapped. "My father is with his other children. What are their names again? Muffy and Fluffy? Flopsie and Mopsie?"

"Sara and Tara," my mother said with a sigh.

I sighed, too. I still hadn't told her that my father's second wife was pregnant with a third kid, maybe a fourth if she popped out twins again. Mom and I lived in the tiny apartment above our garage because we had rented our house to the Loose family to save money. Meanwhile, my father and his new family lived in Arizona, with sunshine and swimming pools and smiling family photos.

Dad had promised me an airline ticket so I could visit them over Christmas vacation. It was the third week in December and the ticket hadn't arrived yet. Sometimes what Dad says and what he does are two very different things.

"Why do you do it, Nick?" Mom said, dabbing tears from her eyes. "Why is everything a joke with you?"

"Why not?" I forced a laugh as my mother blotted runny mascara from her cheeks. "You gotta admit—it saves on tissues and eye makeup."

"You can't joke your way out of everything. Like this thing with the girls' locker room. That crosses the line from immature to"—Mom choked up—"to rude, ignorant behavior. Maybe even criminal. Why did you do it, Nick?"

"I'm sorry, Mom. I'm asking myself the same question." And I had been since 12:05 this afternoon, when I dropped back into this world with a thud.

It was so out-of-the-world weird that there was only one way I would get an answer.

Just as Mike Pillsbury raised weird to an art form, Jill Pillsbury raised popularity to an exact science. Mike's fifteen-year-old sister was the goddess of Ashby Senior High. Even though she was Homecoming Princess, Sophomore Class President, and Honor Society standout, she still had a kind word and a smile for everyone.

Except me.

"What do you want, Freakface?" she snarled as she answered the front door.

"World peace, an end to hunger, and a million bucks." I laughed.

Jill wasn't laughing. Under her bluster, she was fighting back tears.

"Is anything wrong?" I asked.

"Is anything right?"

"Let me guess. You broke up with Sean," I said.

"That was last month's loser," she said. "Eric . . ."

"Right. The Student Council President."

"He thinks he broke up with me. But I was about to end it anyway."

"Anything I can do?" I asked.

"Yeah. Get lost," she said, blowing her nose with a vengeance.

"Want me to beat him silly?" I said. "Better yet, I could smear him senseless."

Jill blinked through the tears. "Huh?"

"Eric-the-Student-Council-Scuzident . . . why do you care what he thinks? Why, that kid is dumber than a box of fishbait."

Jill stared at me like I was nuts. But she stopped sniffling.

"But don't worry—someday Eric will find himself—and wish he hadn't," I said with a straight face. "If ignorance is bliss, Eric is the happiest dude alive."

12

Jill's mouth twisted into a half smile.

"He's loaded with personality—the personality of a toothbrush bristle."

Jill giggled.

"That kid is living proof that man can live without a brain."

"Enough!" Jill laughed. "I'm not done being miserable yet. Go harass my brother. He's up in that infantile treehouse." Jill shoved me out the door.

As I climbed the ladder to the old elm tree, I realized Jill hadn't gone back inside. She stood on the porch, drinking in the winter wind.

She wouldn't drown her sorrows that way. I knew that from experience.

I had spent the best days of my life in Mike's treehouse, listening to the Pillsbury Chronicles. At one time, Mike believed he was an alien, abandoned on Earth. That was his explanation for why he was so smart and so weird. Mike's stories were weird but they were also out-of-this-world awesome. So we didn't mind pretending along with Mike that he might be an alien and that aliens might arrive at any moment.

Then, the aliens did arrive.

It began last Halloween with Ashby's football hero, Scott Schreiber. Scott had a crush on Katelyn Sands, who, for some bizarre reason, liked Mike better even though he's a geek and she's the most popular girl in our class. In typical dumb-jock fashion, Schreiber took revenge on Mike at a school dance.

Humiliated beyond bearing, Mike sent an SOS to the stars through his satellite dish. *Come and get me*, he transmitted. *I don't belong here.*

He got what he asked for.

The aliens came. And they kept coming, from the slimy Bom lawyer to the four-faced Jarm to the helpful Sirian. Just when Mike thought he had convinced them all to go home, the worst of all arrived—the poisonous, monstrous Jong. When the Jong kidnapped little Jay Loose, our five-year-old neighbor, it looked like the end of our world. But Mike, Katelyn, Barnabus the Sirian, and that doofus Schreiber vanquished the Jong, freed his alien captives, and got all the aliens off the planet safely.

Even with snow coming down outside, the tree-house was toasty. Mike had recently insulated it and installed an electric heater.

Before I could even start pouring out my problems, Mike passed judgment on me. "Pervert."

"Who you calling a pervert?" I asked.

"You. How gross can you get, spying on girls in the shower?"

"I did no such thing," I said. "In fact, when the opportunity presented itself, I turned my back and walked away."

"If you weren't spying, what were you doing there?"

I flopped down on the cushion next to Mike and dug into our box of snacks. "You, being the master of all things weird, are gonna love this. Aaron Fleming was about to smash my face in—"

"I heard about that, too," Mike said. "That doofus weighs a hundred and eighty pounds. For a smart kid, you're about as stupid as it gets."

"Not stupid. A risk-taker. Living life on the edge." I washed down a fudge bar with a box of grape juice. "So anyway, just as Aaron was about to pound my lights out, I disappeared."

"Some risk-taker. Make trouble, then run away from it. But that's what you're best at, Nick. Ducking and running."

"You don't get it! I didn't run away. I just disappeared. Poof! One instant I was near my locker, and the next instant I was across the school, in the aerobics room."

"I thought you were in the locker room."

"That was after I had wandered the school for two hours while everyone was frozen."

"Frozen? You mean cold?"

"I mean . . . like a statue," I said. "It was so freaky. Nothing moved, nothing breathed, things suspended in midair. Just like in your Chronicles, Mike."

Mike jumped up. "They're stories!" he shouted.

"Everyone has to stop taking them so seriously!" He dug his math book and calculator out of his backpack.

"What are you doing? You're supposed to be listening to me!"

"I can't discuss this now. I have homework," Mike said.

"But I'm in trouble," I said.

"You're always in trouble, Nick." Mike plopped back down into his beanbag chair and opened his book. "Just keep your mouth shut and keep me out of it."

"Fine," I said, shutting my mouth with a dramatic *click*.

I opened the tarp a crack and stared into the night, watching the plump flakes tumbling down. I supposed I should go home; Mike had made it clear the discussion was over. But it was peaceful up here, listening to the snow softly fall, watching the world turn white. Letting my worries drift away.

Then I heard it. A drum beat, *tap-tap-tapping*, far away, like a parade that is still out of sight. Louder now, not a drum. It was a *pum-pum-pum*. Hoofbeats—like in those old black-and-white westerns on Saturday-morning TV. Closer still, muffled by the snow but *thum-thum-thumming* hard through the patchy brush that bordered the backyards on this side of the street.

"Mike, do you hear that?"

**16**

Mike looked up from his book, his face scrunched in annoyance. "Do you mind? I'm trying to get some work done."

"But don't you hear . . ."

Suddenly, a flash of light cut through me, and, like a shooting star, I tumbled out of the treehouse.

And into midnight.

# 4

THE NiGHT HAD LoST iTS VoiCE. THE world was as frozen as the snow.

I picked myself out of six inches of snow. Six inches? An instant ago, it had been a dusting. Now the snow was over my sneakers. But I felt no cold, and as I took a couple of steps, I left no footprints.

I was here. But not here. Again.

My watch read 8:40 P.M. The clock on Pillsbury's microwave, which I could see through the back kitchen window, read 12:05 A.M. Coincidence? I thought not.

Mike must have seen me disappear but the tree-house was dark. Some best friend—while I was here in this time warp, he was probably upstairs in a warm bed.

I bent down to make a snowball to throw at his window. But my hands whizzed through the snow like it wasn't there.

I strained to listen for any sign of life. Like this morning, the silence was complete. No cars creeping through the snow, no roaring of snow blowers, no creaking of tree limbs.

Nothing.

Weirdest of all was the snow. Each flake hung in midair, fluffy and motionless. As I walked down the driveway to the street, I left no trail. Goose bumps crept up my neck, but not from the cold. The temperature was steady and warm; I could have run around in shorts and not felt anything. The snow hung motionless in the light of the street lamps. I stood in the circle of light and looked behind me.

I didn't even cast a shadow.

I hiked to Ashby Center, in the direction from where I had heard the hoofbeats. At midnight, there wasn't a soul out; the bad weather had kept even the cars off the road. The trees on Ashby Common were laced with white lights that twinkled through the flurries like a million stars.

Had I imagined the hoofbeats? Or was there something in this snowy night with me?

As I window-shopped the stores, little-kid memories flooded me: watching for Santa Claus over the

**19**

rooftops; making a wish list of toys while Mike listed books and science equipment; Christmas caroling at nursing homes and hospitals; hanging my stocking by the chimney with care. I drifted in snow and lights and dreams and—

—stepped through a body lying on the sidewalk!

Why would anyone lie on the sidewalk on a snowy night? Was this dude dead? I needed to call 911. But how could I call 911 when I couldn't even leave a footprint?

The man was bundled in a coat—no, on closer look, he had at least two coats. His head was hidden by a knit hat pulled tight under a doofus cap with earflaps like the one Mike wears on cold days. On his feet were rubber snowmobile boots wrapped in burlap sacks. His hands were covered with mittens and double-wrapped the same way.

I was pretty sure Mr. Burlap was just asleep and not dead, but would I even hear a heartbeat anyway? His face seemed peaceful under the wrappings and wild beard. He wasn't on the sidewalk but on a grate, the kind hot air blows out of.

I thought it was bad living in a cramped apartment. But this guy was sleeping on the street. He had no home; and he couldn't have a family, because they would never let this happen to him. Even when my parents divorced, Mom promised me that my father would never let us be homeless.

Suddenly, I just wanted to go home. Even if it was only a crummy apartment above a garage.

I was crossing the Common when I heard the hoofbeats again. "Hey!" I shouted. "Who's there?"

The *plop-plop* slowed to a walk. I raced toward the sound, my own feet *plopping*, my breath coming harder as I ran faster. Then I stopped. Listened.

Nothing.

"Where are you?" I called. There it was, now a slow *tap-tap-tap*. The street was dark except for one light, casting a small circle on the sidewalk. Beyond the pale light, something moved.

Soft footsteps—one, two, three—then, out of the darkness, a shape. The thing was close enough so I could tell that, whatever it was, it was big.

"Hey," I yelled. "Come here." The shape turned slowly, then passed through the light, showing itself for a brief moment.

A unicorn?

No way! Horses with horns just do not exist, not in this world. The creature was probably a giant dog, coated with snow, or maybe some stray goat from one of the local farms.

"It's okay," I whispered. "Come on back. I won't hurt you."

The shadow shifted toward me.

"That's it, guy." Two silver lights glimmered from

**21**

the snow, like drops of moonlight flickering through a lace curtain. *Goats and dogs do not have stars in their eyes.*

"I won't hurt you," I whispered. "I'm as lost as you are."

The creature stepped back into the light. He was not quite a horse—thinner, the legs too long, the tail too wide, the eyes too sparkling, the face too intelligent.

His hide flowed with light and color, as if he were lit from inside by his own fire. On his forehead was an ivory spiral, pointed to the sky as if searching out the stars.

I reached out, wanting to feel the colors moving under his hide. His silver eyes shifted, locking on to mine. There was something clear and true and terrible in the way he stared me down. Somehow, I knew he was judging me.

I knew I would come up short. I always do.

"I'm sorry," I said. I took my hand away, but I couldn't stop staring. Looking into his eyes, I felt like I was following a silver path, sometimes running away, sometimes running to.

But always running.

After what seemed like an instant or a million lifetimes, the creature blinked. Then, a sudden burst of gold flared in his eyes.

"What?" I said.

The night exploded into flames! Balls of fire

hurtled out of the sky, bursting around us like fire-crackers. The creature reared, then disappeared.

I dove into a hedge. As a storm of fire burst all around, I hugged the ground, praying for the snow that wasn't really there to protect me from the flames that really were. Even though it seemed the hedge couldn't catch fire, I figured I could. I burrowed deeper, listening to the *pound-pound* of hooves. The creature had to be halfway across the Common by now.

I hid forever—at least ten minutes. When I mustered enough courage to come out, the creature was long gone. He could be in Kansas by now, at the speed he had been moving.

Main Street was just as I had left it—a frozen Winter Wonderland. There were no hoofprints in the snow and no scorch marks on the trees or stores.

Who or what had shot the fireballs? Were they aimed at the creature? Or at me? The questions piled up like snow in a blizzard.

I needed answers—answers I was determined to wring out of Albert Michael Pillsbury.

## 5

i SAT ON THE STAiRS, COUNTiNG SNOW-
flakes, listening for hoofbeats, and ducking imaginary missiles. I couldn't get inside the apartment
because I couldn't open the door. As my watch
passed midnight and clicked toward 12:05, a blast of
cold air knocked me against the door. The curtain of
flakes vibrated, then suddenly swirled from the sky.
As the world hummed back into reality, I thudded
back into *now*.

Mom had waited up for me. "Out at this time of
night! On a school night! You could have been hurt.
Killed! Where were you?"

If I told my mother the truth, she'd send me back
to the shrink I had to go to after the divorce. So I
shrugged. "Here. There. Everywhere. What does it
matter?"

"What does it matter? What would I do if I lost you, too?" Mom burst into tears and disappeared into her tiny bedroom.

I disappeared into my own room. The walk-in closet in my half sisters' nursery in Arizona was bigger than the bedroom I had inherited after my parents' divorce.

*Dissolution of property*, the courts had called it. I had wondered what the legal term for the dissolution of my life was. Then I realized that I already knew.

Divorce.

I lay down on my bed. My head spun with colors—a silver path, leading everywhere; red-hot fire, flickering everywhere; dark night, stretching everywhere. I blinked away the colors and stared at the peeling paint on my ceiling. White flakes, just hanging there . . .

*The sky filled with white flakes. Snow, I thought, but it's too hot to snow. And then my heart ignited with terror because I realized it wasn't snow—it was ash.*

*The world burned. Trees, houses, grass—all blazed with white-hot flames. I ran down the street, breathing in ash and smoke, shouting, "Fire!"*

*But nothing moved. The night was silent except for the crackling of fire.*

*Then I saw her—and screamed. Jill's hair was on fire! No, not fire, just her deep red hair reflecting the hot flames.*

*Jill stared at me. There was something clear and true and terrible in the way she stared me down. Somehow, I knew she was judging me.*

*And I knew I would fall short. I always do. "I'm sorry," I said. "I really am."*

*"Don't be stupid," she said, grabbing my hand. "Get me out of here."*

*Everything but the pavement was burning. We ran as fast as we could but I knew we only had a minute before it would swallow us up.*

*A shadow passed in front of us, almost too fast to be seen.*

*"Wait!" I yelled at the shape. "Slow down!"*

*The shadow flickered, a cool spot among the flames.*

*"Help us!" I yelled. "Give us a ride."*

*The horned horse reared, his moonlight eyes turning impossibly cold in this blazing world.*

*"I bend my back to no one!" he bellowed. In a flash, he was gone.*

*And in a flash, the fire swallowed us.*

Breakfast was a sorry affair. As Mom buttered toast and scrambled eggs, she kept glancing over her shoulder at me. Her face shifted between anger, fear, and sadness. I wanted to ask what *the matter* was, but I already knew the answer.

I was *the matter*.

As I dug into my eggs, Mom poured a cup of

coffee and sat down with me. "Nick, I have some troubling news."

"Yeah," I mumbled, chewing my toast as if I didn't care.

"It's about your father."

I almost choked. "What's wrong with Dad?"

"He's okay. But his company isn't doing well. People were laid off."

"Dad got canned?"

"No, he still has his position. But he had to take a cut in pay. And they're requiring him to work longer hours to cover the people who were let go. He knows he promised you a trip to Arizona for Christmas . . ."

"Let me guess. He can't afford the airline ticket."

"I'm afraid not," Mom said.

I slammed down my juice. "Why didn't he tell me himself? Was he too chicken?"

Mom's eyes narrowed. "He tried. But you weren't here when he called last night. You were, as you put it, *out*." Mom slammed down her coffee cup next to my juice glass.

"I'm sorry," I mumbled. I grabbed my dish to head for the sink. Mom grabbed my hand and guided me back into my seat.

"I'm sorry, Nick. I wish I could buy you the ticket, but you know . . ."

Yes, I knew. Mom did all she could to keep a roof over our head, even if it was a crummy

**27**

garage apartment roof.

"It's okay, Mom." I smiled and kissed her forehead. The kiss was real, but the smile was fake and both of us knew it.

Just like both of us knew it wasn't okay.

## 6

THERE ARE TWO WORDS THAT STRIKE joy into any kid's heart. These two words can make the sun shine even when the sky is gray and Arizona is too far away.

NO SCHOOL.

The storm had continued all night, leaving behind a foot of snow and a day off from school. I grabbed my boots, jacket, and gloves, and skied down the stairs.

Mike met me in his backyard. "Where did you go last night?" he asked.

"You tell me," I said. "You know something."

"So do you," Mike said. "But what?"

"I don't know," we said in unison.

"We'd better find out," Mike said.

Moments later we settled into the treehouse.

Outside, the wind howled. Inside, we were already sweating; the heater cranked on high.

Mike's stories of aliens had a way of coming true. I needed to know what story was rattling in his brain right now—and if I was a lead character in it. "Tell me your latest story," I said.

"You started this," Mike said. "So you go first."

I explained again about getting bounced into a time warp where time stood still but I didn't. Then I described a creature that didn't quite look like a horse and maybe looked like a unicorn but definitely was nothing from this world.

When I started in with the fireballs, Mike turned as white as the snow piled up outside. "This is too weird, even for me," he said. "We'd better just let it go." He jumped out of his beanbag and headed for the ladder.

I grabbed him back. "You took on a fleet of space-ships, but you can't handle a little story?"

"A *little* story? I hope to heck that's all it is." Mike sat back down, took a deep breath, and began.

*Imagine being able to run like the wind. I don't mean so fast that other kids can't keep up, or so fast that you can outrun a dog or a cheetah or even an automobile. I mean so fast that you sweep across the countryside in a blink.*

*So fast that you're here, and then in an instant, you're there.*

**30**

*Resembling our Earth horses, the Zephyrs were intelligent creatures of power and grace that lived on the garden planet of Grayle. As notorious as the Zephyrs were for their incredible speed, they were more known for their stubborn hearts and bucking backs.*

"I bend my back to no one," I mumbled.

"How did you know that?"

"No clue." I shrugged. "How do you know the things *you* do?"

"No clue. I just do." Mike took another deep breath, then continued.

*Discipline is a hard master. Human children squirm in their seats as their teachers instruct them; the Bom young blow noxious bubbles when their elders pontificate on the law; even the sweet-natured Hanzels float away when being lectured by a parent.*

*The Zephyrs refused any instruction or discipline. Instead, they frolicked their days away, not bothering to understand that starvation was coming because of their lack of self-control. Grayle was filled with grassy plains and blooming fruit trees, but as the years went on, the Zephyrs ate their way across the continents, never giving back to their home planet what they thoughtlessly took.*

*Grayle was rare in that it had spawned two intelligent races. The Garths were slugs—rude, stupid, and without ambition, resembling humans. Their* eyes were dull, their backs shaggy, and their hands large and clumsy. They resisted labor and spent their days lounging in low-hanging trees, munching on leaves and daydreaming. Though they shared Grayle with the Zephyrs, they couldn't be bothered to say hello, let alone work together to save themselves and their planet.

The Draconians from the neighboring constellation of Draco went to galactic court, demanding guardianship over Grayle. "Those worthless races are ruining the planet!" they complained. "We need to banish them and take over."

The Sirians begged for the opportunity to help the Garths and Zephyrs grow up.

"You can't teach a sack of potatoes to grow up!" yelled the Draconians. "You can't tell the wind to change its course!"

With the argumentative Boms representing both sides of the case, it dragged on forever. The Draconians got sick of waiting. What the courts were unwilling to give, the Draconians simply decided to take.

Warships filled the skies of Grayle, spitting laser fire like exploding hail. The Zephyrs fled at incredible speeds, but wherever they went, the fire followed them. The Garths burrowed into their trees but the flames swept through, forcing them out of hiding.

When the Draconians had driven the surviving Garths and Zephyrs into a valley, the invaders left

**32**

*their ships and went planetside to finish their house-cleaning.*

*The Zephyrs and Garths, who had never even acknowledged each other's existence, now cowered together as troops surrounded them. With heavy scales, thrashing tails, and clawed hands, the soldiers from the stars struck terror into their irresponsible hearts.*

*One Garth, with an ounce more initiative than a worm, scaled a small tree, hoping to find shelter. The soldiers laughed, spitting hot embers everywhere.*

*One young Zephyr bucked in fear against the tree. The terrified Garth tumbled out of the tree, onto the Zephyr's back.*

*It was as if lightning had struck the Zephyr and the Garth.*

*A bolt of massive power ran through them, energizing them from head to toe, mane to tail. Legend says it was their destiny finding its fulfillment. The Zephyr, who submitted to no one, bent his back to the Garth. The Garth, who climbed no higher than the nearest green bush, rose on the back of the Zephyr.*

*Together, they charged the troops—a lone knight on a lone steed. With no armor and no weapon, they trampled down the fire-breathers. Within seconds, each Zephyr bent for a Garth rider. Together they banished the invaders, reclaimed their homeland, and embraced their destiny.*

**33**

*Since that fateful battle, the two races have bonded together as a galactic force for good. When someone is needed to keep the peace, relieve the oppressed, or vanquish evil, a brave Garth, riding on a speedy and strong Zephyr, follows the golden path to What Is Right.*

"But what about the horn?" I said. "The horse-guy I saw can't be a Zephyr. He had a horn."

"Like a unicorn," Mike said. "Mythic creatures that don't exist."

"Right. Like aliens don't exist," I snapped.

"Okay, you've got a point. So the question is, what is this unicorn-creature you saw? An alien? A rare Earth species? A mythic creature? Or some being from another dimension that doesn't exist in time?"

"I don't know! You're supposed to know these things," I yelled. "You're the expert on all things weird."

"Don't you get it, Nick? I don't know any more than you do! I used to dream about aliens coming to Earth. Now it's all one big nightmare. I wish they'd all just go away." Mike covered his face with his hands.

"Hey, man, you can't make it go away. Gotta deal with it, right? That's what you're always nagging me about."

Mike peered through his fingers. His eyes drooped with worry. "No matter what, we stick together?"

"No matter what," I swore.

"Easy to say now. But wait until some ticked-off alien has his claws around your throat. You gonna joke him to death?"

"Die laughing," I snorted as I rubbed my throat.

# 7

I WAS COOL BEYOND COOL. WHAT OTHER seventh grader has his own staff of bodyguards, sworn to protect every pimple on his scrawny face?

The next day in school, Mike assigned Katelyn, Scott, Stacia Caraviello, and himself to stay with me every minute. Because Earth had been deemed unready for alien contact, we couldn't go to the police or army for help. Revealing the existence of the aliens that swarm through the universe could bring neutralization upon our whole planet.

So the chore of watching for the horned horse and trying to keep me out of a time warp fell on the only humans who had had actual contact with aliens. Mike and Katelyn had faced off against the evil Jong when he had kidnapped Jay Loose. A month later, Mike had helped Scott and Stacia save the singing alien, the Lyra, from the menacing Shards.

Okay, we were just seventh graders. But we were all Earth had.

After homeroom, I was banished to the Academic Center, where I was serving my in-house suspension. Scott Schreiber arrived minutes later, armed with his football helmet and a fire extinguisher. "I hope I get to go with you," he whispered. "I'm awesome at fighting off alien invasions."

Stacia relieved Scott in second period. Mike had told me she was famous; she had played her violin all over the world for thousands of people. Schreiber used to call her a Weird Band Girl until he got to know her. She didn't look like a football hero's girlfriend, with her flyaway brown hair, chubby cheeks, and granny glasses.

In third period, Katelyn slid next to me and squeezed my hand. "I knew you weren't a pervert," she said.

"No, you didn't," I said.

"Well, I *hoped* you weren't a pervert. I'm so glad there's a perfectly reasonable—well, okay, perfectly weird—explanation for your being in the girls' locker room."

Guilt twisted my insides. While I wasn't actually a pervert, there had been a scummy part of me that had intended to spy on the girls. Katelyn squeezed my hand again, and I was suddenly happy that I

**37**

had kicked my scummy side into the shower drain and had walked away.

When Mike came in at the start of fourth period, Mrs. Flack, the academic advisor, greeted him like he was a celebrity. Which he kind of is, if you're a teacher and love genius geeks. Once Mike was satisfied that there were no Draconians hanging from the sprinkler system, he sat down at my table.

"So, have you figured it out yet?" I whispered. "Why they keep coming, even though Earth is off-limits to aliens?"

"I think that's why they keep coming," Mike said. "Because Earth is not part of the Galactic Federation, it's a good place for aliens in trouble to hide. And the aliens come specifically to us because they know we want to help."

"So it's a good thing they're coming, right?" I asked. "So we can help them?"

Mike dropped his head onto the table. "I don't know," he mumbled. "How many seventh-graders does it take to save the planet?"

I laughed. "As many as it takes to screw in a light bulb?"

"You haven't been tested yet," Mike snapped. "Wait until you see your life passing before your eyes. Think you'll laugh then?"

"It beats the alternative."

"What's that?" Mike asked.

"Crying," I said.

"Are you serious?"

"Am I ever serious?" I said, then dropped my face to the table so Mike couldn't see that I was.

After lunch, Jill Pillsbury strolled into the Academic Center like she owned the place. With her flashy hair, tight jeans, and Homecoming-Princess smile, she turned every head.

"What's she doing here?" Mike and I asked at the same time.

Jill whispered something to Mrs. Flack, then came over to our table. She poked Mike. "You're relieved, bookworm," she said.

"But . . ." Mike stuttered. "I'm supposed to be helping Nick."

"Outta here, Albert. I'm taking over."

My heart beat like a hammer. "What are you doing here?" I asked. "Slumming?"

"An Honor Society project," Jill said. "We've been assigned to the Middle School to help tutor. I get to choose my victim, and Nick is always good for a laugh. So get lost, Mike."

Mike stared at me, silently willing me to tell Jill to take a hike. But heck—why sit next to a geek when I could sit with a goddess? Mike had my safety at heart, but Jill had amazing red hair, a killer smile, and tight jeans.

"Go ahead," I said. "I'll keep Jill-the-Pill out of trouble."

"Are you nuts?" Mike hissed.

"You don't have to sit in my lap to watch me," I hissed back.

Mike frowned, then grabbed his backpack. He went to the next table and opened the physics book that he reads when he's bored. He kept one eye on Albert Einstein and the other on Jill and me.

Jill slid in so close to me that I got dizzy from her scent. That must be what was making my heart pound so hard—an allergic reaction to all that sweet shampoo and perfume and general Jillness.

"So is Eric still in the trash can?" I asked.

"Him? He's in the landfill, all plowed under and long forgotten." Jill laughed. Mrs. Flack looked our way. Jill opened a book and motioned me closer.

"There's a new guy in school," she whispered.

"What? Here?" I asked.

"Be serious. At the high school." She beamed. "You should see him. Blond hair, blue eyes, great shoulders—"

"Like I want to hear about this month's flavor of boyfriend?" I asked with a huge yawn.

"Come on, Freakface." Jill put her arm around me and pulled me close. "I'm just bursting. I have to tell someone."

I rolled my eyes. "Well, since I haven't done my good deed for the day . . . what's Mr. Perfection's name?"

"Troy. Isn't it such a great name?" She sighed.

"And what rock did Troy Terrific crawl out from under?"

"Someplace far away." Jill twisted in her seat. "Hey! What's that?"

"What's what?" I asked.

"That noise."

Now I heard it, a *tap-tap-tap* that in a couple of heartbeats became a *thum-thum-thum*, then a *pound-pound-pound*.

Hoofbeats.

"You can hear that?" I asked, but Jill was already on her way to the door. As I jumped up to follow, I glanced back at Mike. His nose was still buried in his book.

"Mike!" I hissed. "Hear it?"

Mrs. Flack scowled. "Where do you two think you're going?"

Jill ignored her and stepped into the hall. As I followed her, I got one last look at Mike. He was rising from his seat, his face filled with alarm. "Hear what?" he asked. "I don't hear anything."

*Now is a good time to go back*, I told myself as the hoofbeats thundered through the halls of Ashby Middle School.

But as Jill tumbled into a flash of light, I grabbed her hand and followed her into midnight.

# 8

HERE WE GO AGAIN, i THOUGHT AS i tumbled out onto a stone floor.

I looked around in surprise. We had warped clear across town to the mall, and landed in the Food Court. A few people huddled over French fries and chicken wings, frozen with their food halfway to their mouths.

Jill shattered the silence with a scream. "No one's moving!" she shrieked.

"We gotta talk." I pulled Jill along until I found a table with two chairs pulled out enough for us to sit on.

"What did you do to me?" she cried. "And what did you do to all these people?"

I breathed deeply, then tried to begin. "You know how Mike is always telling stories about aliens?"

"What does that idiot have to do with this?"

Panicked tears streamed down her face. She sniffled, then reached for the napkin dispenser that was on the table between us.

She pulled at a napkin. The napkin was as unmoving as a mountain. "You little creep!" she yelled. "What did you do to me?"

"I didn't do anything," I yelled back. Then I lowered my voice and tried to sound reasonable. "Jill, you have to understand, there are things that happen in this world . . . this universe, that are, well . . . out of this world. And just like Mike tells in his stories, they happen right here. Right on this planet. Right in this little town."

Jill's face turned almost as red as her hair. But she kept quiet long enough for me to tell her about how Mike, Scott, Stacia, Katelyn, Jay, and I had been involved with aliens for months now.

When I finally paused to get a breath, Jill laughed. "Good one, Nick. That story's almost as creative as one of my brother's fantasies."

She jumped from her chair and ran to the nearest diner, a truck driver type sipping a cola. "Hey, Mister," Jill yelled. "Joke's over. You can move now." When the truck driver type didn't blink, Jill poked his arm.

Her hand went right through him. Jill went down on her knees in a near faint.

"Jill, we can't change anything," I said as I helped her up. "We're in a time warp."

"Time warp?" she mumbled. "I was hoping it was a dream."

"Pretend it is." I forced a laugh. "What kids don't dream of having the mall to themselves?"

Jill tightened her arms around my neck. I didn't know if she was hanging on for dear life or trying to strangle me. "Swear it. This is the truth?" she said.

"Yes," I said, stifling the urge to crack a joke.

"So there really are"— Jill gulped—"extraterrestrials?"

"Lots of them," I replied. "And Mike and I think that somehow they're involved in this time warp thing."

"Then what are we waiting for? We have to call the police!"

I sat her down again and explained how we couldn't tell the authorities. Official notification before the planet is ready to join the federation could result in neutralization.

"What's neutralization?" Jill asked.

"You don't want to know," I whispered.

"So now what?"

I grinned. "Shop till we drop?"

Brave midnight shoppers were scattered throughout the mall, loaded with bags and boxes. I could almost catch the thoughts frozen in their heads. *Did I buy the right gift? How am I going to pay for all this?* One store clerk was caught in mid-yawn, her weary silence speaking loud and clear: *My feet are killing me.*

A grandmother type rested on a bench, watching the world go by with a sparkle in her eyes. *Peace on earth and goodwill to men.*

Jill stopped at a display of sweaters. "Cashmere," she said, trying to pick one up. It wouldn't budge.

"I told you before—you can't move it," I said. "You're not really here."

"That's right. I am out of here!" She pushed past me, running back into the concourse.

"Jill!" I panted. "Wait."

She was on a beeline for the main entrance and nothing was going to stop her. At least, not until she flung herself against the door and bounced back onto her butt. I couldn't even offer to help her up—I was in serious danger of puking my oxygen-starved brains out.

"They locked us in," she said.

"It's not locked. We just can't change anything," I said. "Not until we get back to *now*."

Jill looked like I had just slapped her. My heart beat harder than ever.

"I'm sorry," I whispered. "I'm sorry I dragged you into this."

Suddenly a dark shadow flitted overhead. Like a small fighter plane with pointed wings, the shadow darted from a beam in the arched ceiling. It dove at us like a bird of prey racing for its kill.

"Run!" I screamed, but Jill was already halfway down the escalator, taking six steps at once.

I finally caught up with her at the Food Court. "Down," I whispered, pushing her under a table.

The shadow swept through the Food Court with a slow *flap-flap*, searching us out. We both gasped, trying to keep our huffing from giving us away.

*Flap-flap.* The thing swept in circles. It knew we were in the Food Court but apparently it couldn't spot us from above. After a minute, the silence returned.

"It's gone," Jill said, starting to crawl out from the table.

I yanked her back. "It's landed."

Sure enough, a delicate *tap-tap* came from about ten tables over. *Tap-tap*, then silence. Then *tap-tap*, closer this time.

"It's looking for us," I whispered.

"We need a weapon," Jill hissed.

"We can't move anything!" I hissed back, so loud that Jill slapped her hand over my mouth.

"Except for things that are on our bodies!" she whispered, patting her shirt.

Great. I could spear the monster with my house key, bribe it with three bucks, or bore it with a breath mint.

*Tap-tap.* The bird of prey was only two tables away. I could see its feet, more lizardlike than

**46**

birdlike; longer and wider than a skateboard, tipped with sharp claws.

*Tap-tap*. One table away.

"Get ready to run," I whispered.

"Where to?" she said.

*Tap-tap*. Too late now. The thing thrust its face under our table. The beast was hung with scales as thick and prickly as a cactus. Its long jaw reminded me of an alligator's, but no alligator has teeth six inches long.

"A dragon," Jill breathed.

"Mike's Draconians . . ." I added.

The creature closed its mouth. I was happy to see those teeth disappear—until I saw the smoke curling out of its nostrils. Its eyes narrowed, and it moved its snout closer.

I decided to tough it out. "Smoking will kill you," I said. Die laughing, right?

"Say something, you LizardPuke!" Jill shouted. "What do you want?"

But the creature stayed silent. Staring. Thinking. Deciding.

I glanced at my watch. Still nine hours before we would hum into *now* and at least have a chair to throw at the beast.

The creature would barbecue us for sure way before then.

The silence was heavy now, like a rock pressing on us. It stretched forever—until I heard a familiar crackle. I glanced at the Burger Blast to see if time had resumed and food was cooking. No, time was still frozen. But somewhere nearby, something sizzled.

"Oh, shoot," I yelped.

The creature opened its mighty mouth, showing the fire brewing in the back of its throat.

"Run!" I yelled.

"Drop dead!" Jill yelled, and whipped something out of her back pocket. With a flick of her trigger finger, Jill maced the creature in the eyes with hair spray. As it went down, it barfed a fireball along the floor.

We ran for our lives, the fire licking at our heels.

# 9

WE SLOWED TO A PANTING CRAWL
two miles later at Ashby Center. We had escaped the
mall through an open window in the men's room.

"Oh, cripes," Jill said, slumping against the
stone wall that bordered Ashby Common. "I'm not
dreaming, am I?"

"Nope," I huffed, my lungs turning inside out.

"Which means my brother is either a genius . . ."

"Yep," I panted.

". . . or a lunatic."

"Yep to that, too."

"He brought all these aliens here?"

"Not all of them," I said. "Just a batch that
wanted to either save or enslave him. But now that
the gate has been opened to the stars, these guys
keep leaking in."

"Wait until I tell Mom and Dad. They're going to . . ." She paused, reading the sour look on my face. "We can't tell anyone, can we?"

"Yep," I said. "I mean, nope. Unless you want the whole planet to be neutralized."

"So, what do we do?"

"We have to catch the Zephyr," I said.

"What's that, some kind of disease?"

"If Mike is right, the Zephyr is a horselike alien. Remember the hoofbeats we heard in school, right before we flipped into this time warp? Somehow the Zephyr is involved. I don't know how, but—"

"Don't sweat it," Jill snapped. "We'll figure it out."

"What's this 'we' stuff?"

"You don't think I'd leave something this important to a Geekface and a Freakface?"

Mike wasn't going to like this, but I wasn't the one who had dragged Jill into this.

Mike could blame the universe for that one.

Main Street was still a Winter Wonderland. As we walked under the lights, Jill's face melted into a kid's grin. "It's like when I was little," she said. "Lights and singing and cookies. Dreaming of dolls and ponies—"

"Forget ponies," I said. "Do you know anything about unicorns?"

"Unicorns were thought to be wild creatures,

hard to subdue except by a pure maiden. And their horns are supposed to have great healing powers. They don't exist, of course."

I laughed. "Right. Just like dragons don't exist."

Our eyes scanned the sky, the trees, the rooftops, alert for fiery sparks or drifting smoke. So much for peace on Earth.

We had gone about a quarter of a mile when Jill jumped over something on the sidewalk. "What is that?" she yelped.

Burlap was back in his usual spot on the grate. "It's okay," I said. "I tripped over—I mean, *through*—him a couple of nights ago. He's not dead, just sleeping."

"On the sidewalk?" she said.

"Beats the alternative," I said.

"What's that?" Jill asked.

"I don't know. And I don't want to know."

"Well, I do know. This guy needs to get to the homeless shelter," Jill said.

"In Ashby?"

"Yeah. There's one in the basement of St. Mark's Church."

"You're kidding. Why do we have a homeless shelter in Ashby?" I asked.

"Because we have homeless people in Ashby," she said. "We're not immune to the real world just because we're a small town. People suffer here, too."

I knew all too well that people suffered in Ashby.

**51**

I just didn't like to talk about it.

"Come on, Nick. We have to figure out how to get this guy there."

"We can't move him until we get back to *now*." I checked my watch. "And that's still hours away," I said.

Jill grabbed my wrist to check the time. "We can't leave him here for the next six hours."

"It's not hours to him. It's only a moment."

"I'm in the Honor Society, Nick. I have to do something. It's my duty." Her eyes were determined.

"You got anything to write on? Or write with?" I asked.

Jill whipped a tube of lipstick out of her jeans pocket. First hair spray, then lipstick. How did she fit it all into those tight pants?

"What are you gawking at, Freakface?"

"Sorry," I said.

Jill uncapped the lipstick and tried to write on the newspaper under the sleeping man's head. Nothing appeared.

"I don't get it!" She rubbed the lipstick on her hand and red appeared. "It's driving me nuts—why can I write on my hand, but not on the newspaper?"

"Mike and I think that when we're in this time warp—bounced into the future—we're not really here. Not yet, anyway. For example, take today. We got bounced out of time during fourth period. Probably around eleven A.M. We got bounced ahead in time—somehow—and arrived at the mall at five minutes after midnight. But until you and I have lived through our own thirteen hours between the time we left and the time when we arrived, we're not really in *now*."

"So we can't do anything to help this guy?"

I unrolled my mints and put the wrapping in my palm. "This paper came with us. So try writing on it."

I held my hand steady while Jill wrote "Go to St. Mark's."

"Now what?" she asked. "The paper's not here yet, really. So we can drop it on this Burlap guy. But if we do that, it'll just blow away when . . . when *now* comes back."

"I know what might work," I said. "But this is going to be mega-creepy." I reached through the man's hand . . . almost swept away in a hurricane of shivers . . . and put the paper under his fingers. "Maybe it will still be here when he wakes up. Maybe he'll read it and go over and get a warm bed."

"And maybe pigs fly." Jill sighed.

"Better pigs than dragons." I laughed.

But I kept my eye on the sky, just in case.

# 10

TWO POLICE CARS WERE PARKED IN
front of our houses. "The cops are looking for us," I
said.

"They think we were kidnapped," Jill said.

"Or they're here to arrest us. Remember, curfew
for kids under sixteen is eleven o'clock."

Jill smacked me. "Thanks a lot, Nick. Hanging
with you has truly expanded my opportunities."

Through the front window, we could see Jill's
parents, Pam and Dana Pillsbury, huddled in serious conversation with three policemen. Usually,
Pam was smart enough to run the world and Dana
was bold enough to try, but they looked pretty shaky
at that moment.

My mom sat nearby, her face buried in crumpled
tissue. Mike stood against the wall, his eyes far

away. Watching for us, I knew.

"Mom! Dad! I'm here!" Jill yelled.

"No, you're not," I shouted. "You won't be here for another five hours."

"So what do we do?" She groaned.

"There's always the mall." I snorted. She punched me.

"Let's find a place to sit down," Jill said with a sigh.

"The treehouse?" I suggested. If the tarp was open, we'd be able to get in.

"Oh, please."

"Would you prefer a grate?"

"Point taken." Jill dragged me through the gate and into the backyard.

I climbed the ladder and slipped sideways through the partially open tarp. I flopped onto the beanbag. Strange; it held me but didn't shift for my weight. I had to slump into Mike's shape—he had sat in it last. The kid had a skinny butt; I needed to shimmy to get comfortable. Meanwhile, Jill stretched out on the sleeping bag.

I eyed our stash of goodies. I fingered the snack cakes, now as immovable as a mountain. My stomach growled like a roaring tiger.

"Shut up," Jill murmured. Her eyes fluttered, then slipped shut.

Nothing to do but wait, so I let my eyes close, too.

*Jill and I rode into the sunset. We rode with the wind, outrunning Eric-the-Student-Council-President and Mr. Goodrich and the Draconians and doubts and fears and Sara and Tara and even Troy, because I was Jill's knight on the white horse now.*

*We ran so fast, we left the wind behind. And then we caught the sun! Before it could slip into the night we rode into it, a blazing ball of fire.*

*"Stop!" I screamed at my horse. "I order you to stop now!"*

*"I bend my back to no one!" He reared, tossing us into the wall of fire.*

*The sun set into the night, taking us with it. The night was dark and icy cold and I knew that I hadn't outrun my fears and doubts.*

*I had been swallowed whole by them.*

"Nick, wake up!" Jill shook me.

I was freezing. "What's happening?" I muttered, trying to shake myself warm.

"We fell asleep," Jill said. She stamped her feet and rubbed her arms.

With impossible effort, I lifted my arm and looked at my watch. It was 1:14 A.M. We had dozed off in the treehouse, come back to *now* without realizing it, and spent almost an hour in the freezing cold without coats.

When we staggered into the Pillsbury house, Dana and Pam smothered Jill in hugs and kisses. My mother slurped all over me; I was still so cold that her tears felt hot on my face.

While everyone was hollering and crying, Mike mouthed something from his corner. *Does she know?*

I quietly nodded.

Mike slumped into a chair as if the weight of the universe had just collapsed on him.

We spent the morning with the magistrate from Youth Services. We were charged with truancy, because they thought we had cut school. The second charge was breaking curfew, because we didn't return home until after 1 A.M.

I snorted, Mom sobbed, Jill steamed, and Dana Pillsbury schmoozed. Each time Jill tried to plead innocent, Mike stomped on her foot and whispered "Neutralization." For our misdeeds, we were sentenced to a week of community service at St. Mark's Shelter for Indigents.

"What's an indigent?" I asked Mike.

"People without permanent addresses. Like these aliens who keep ending up on our doorsteps," he said.

"What're we going to do about the aliens?" I asked.

"You have to call for help."

"Me?" I squealed. "You're the expert!"

"I'm also on galactic probation. I swore I'd never call outer space again. So you need to do it," Mike said.

"But how? I'm not the techno-brain you are."

"I can't even give you a hint," Mike said. "I don't dare be implicated in this. But if Scott Schreiber figured out how to do it all by himself, certainly you can."

Mike and I entered school on a late pass. I spent the rest of the day in the Academic Center, listening for hoofbeats and trying to figure out how to contact the Sirians. The doglike aliens were compassionate and brave, but they were impossible to get hold of. Why didn't they get a one-eight-hundred number like everyone else? Just because they were a non-profit intergalactic relief organization didn't mean they had to be cheap.

Mike had contacted the aliens through his satellite dish. It had been a feat of technical genius and invention. When Scott Schreiber needed help from the stars, he used what resources he had—his fame as a football player—and put out his call for help during a television interview.

I was smarter than Schreiber by a light-year, but I was still no genius. And no one was going to interview me on television.

After lunch I logged on to the Internet to research snake molting for science class. When Mrs. Flack went out for coffee, I hopped on to my favorite website.

eSWAP. Buy, sell, trade.

I was cruising the comic book listings when I had

a brainstorm. You could get *anything* on eSWAP. Maybe even help from outer space. I logged on to my account and began typing.

Wanted: Sirius help. I am plagued by a Zephyr with a commitment problem and a lizard with breath so bad it burns paint off walls. I've been hit with every penalty but death . . . afraid that's next. Please help. Respond to Freakface@lifeisajoke.com

My finger lingered over the ENTER key. Did I dare send this? Did I dare not to? Maybe I should just roll myself in burlap and lie low for a while. But trouble always seemed to find me. Why not strike first?

I pressed ENTER and held my breath as my plea for help whizzed into cyberspace. And, I hoped, beyond.

# 11

**ST. MARK'S SHELTER FOR INDIGENTS**
smelled worse than my socks on gym day.

"I think it's cabbage soup." Jill wrinkled her nose. "My mother made it for a week straight during her fiber-will-save-the-world kick."

The smell was nauseatingly familiar; I mentally compared it to everything from sour milk to dog poop, but somehow I couldn't quite place it.

Dana Pillsbury, who had driven us to the shelter, worked his way through the tables of hungry people like a politician at a fund-raiser. "How're ya doing?" he said to a shaggy-haired hippie.

"Groovy!" The Hippie Guy grinned, all gums and no teeth.

As Jill and I rushed past, the Hippie Guy gave us the peace sign.

"Yeah, groovy," I muttered, trying to keep up with Dana, who always moved at the speed of light. I got an ache in my chest, missing my own father, who always moved slowly enough for me to keep up.

Except when he left us and moved to Arizona.

A booming voice knocked me out of my pity party. "Welcome!" Our host looked like Santa Claus—white beard, apple cheeks, and rolling belly. "I'm the shelter director," he said. "Quin's the name. No Mister necessary. Nice to see you. Hungry? Or perhaps you need beds for the night?"

"Beds? Why do you ask that? Do we look like we need a bed?" Jill asked in a hurt tone.

Quin laughed. "Yes, you do."

Jill's eyes went wide. "We do?"

Quin gently took her arm. "I'm trying to make a point, Miss Pillsbury."

"You know my name?"

"Yes, and I know why you're here."

"Then you know that I don't . . . need your services," she said.

"Not today, you don't. But do you think that *any* of our clients expect to end up here? They're people like you or me—someone's husband or daughter or aunt. Sure, sometimes they're misfits, but sometimes they're sick and too often they've just hit some nasty luck," Quin said. "Regardless of why anyone's here, we treat everyone the same."

"The same—how the same?" I asked.

"Like we would want to be treated. With courtesy and caring. Are you kids up for that?"

Jill looked at Dana, then me. "I'm an Honor Society member. Absolutely."

Quin turned to me. "And what about you, Mr. Thorpe? Can you put up with us for a week?"

"Hey. Free food and all the floors you can scrub. Who can pass up that bargain?" I said.

"Sounds like you kids are in good hands." Dana glanced at his watch. "I'll pick you up at nine o'clock."

Jill glanced around the room. More people had come in now, wrapped in shaggy coats, trash bags, and crazy hats. "Dad . . ." she called.

"Yes, Jill?" Dana said.

"Drive carefully. It's slippery out there." She grabbed my hand and squeezed it so tightly I almost gasped. I didn't care—somehow a little pain from Jill Pillsbury actually felt good.

Supper was lasagna, and it smelled like heaven. Quin left Jill in the kitchen to help his mother, Ivy, in making salad. Unlike her Kris Kringle son, Ivy Quin looked like she had just stepped off a beach—tan, slim, silver-blond. *Forty years ago*, I thought, *she must have been Miss America or a film star*. Even up to her elbows in carrots, she was glamorous.

Quin then escorted me to the men's shower room, where the cabbage soup stink was strong enough to peel the tiles off the walls.

"What is that?" I choked.

"No clue." Quin opened a tiny window high on the wall. Cold air flooded in. "It started last night. We emptied all the trash containers and scrubbed them out this morning. Checked all the food to make sure nothing had spoiled. We even checked the clients' lockers—sometimes they hoard food."

"Lockers?"

"To protect what little our clients do own." Quin handed me a bucket stuffed with heavy rubber gloves, a scrub brush, and disinfectant. "We've got to keep working on this smell, or our clients will be sleeping outside in the freezing cold just to escape it."

"Why don't you make them come in when they do that?" I asked. "Couldn't they, like, freeze to death?"

"Yes, they can. And sometimes they do," Quin said. "But unless they're very sick or breaking the law, we can't make anyone do anything."

"I won't bend my back to anyone," I whispered.

"What?"

"Um, nothing," I said quickly. "I guess I just don't get it."

Quin shrugged. "What's there to get? It's not always a nice world, son."

"Oh," I said. What else could I say? *I found this guy Burlap sleeping on a grate but I couldn't get him help because I was in a time warp, chasing after a unicorn and being chased by a LizardPuke. So I left him sleeping in the cold, not-so-nice world.*

If I started talking like that, they'd send me to someplace scarier than a homeless shelter.

The shelter wasn't what I expected; even though it was in the basement of a church, it was wide-open and neat. The dining room was half the size of a gym, with spotless tables and plenty of plastic chairs. The kitchen was cluttered but clean.

To get to the shower room, we had come through the men's bunkroom. It was lined with cots, the pillows covered with bright white cases and the gray blankets all tightly tucked in. Quin said there was a room similar to it for the ladies and their young children. It wasn't the worst place in the world.

Until a glob of slime dropped into my cleaning bucket.

"Gross!" I yelped. Bobbing in the soapsuds, the goo was green with purple highlights. Something jarred in my brain. That smell—worse than dog sweat, cat puke, or rotting fish guts—that smell was one I had encountered in Mike Pillsbury's bedroom back in October, after his first meeting with an alien.

"I know a Bom when I smell one." I looked up. The basement ceiling was high, dark, and laced with pipes. "Come on down from there!"

A tentacle snaked its way down the shower head. Then there was a heavy *plop*.

My heart flip-flopped as a slug the size of a stuffed chair quivered in front of me. I hadn't ever met a Bom, but Mike's description was accurate—a smelly blob, covered with slime. Around the Bom's neck hung the small translator box that allowed creatures from any star system to converse with anyone else.

"Welcome to Earth and all that," I said, trying not to puke. It wasn't the Boms' fault that they were aromatically challenged. They probably smelled like springtime to each other.

"You are the Freakface?" the creature said in a deep, rolling voice.

eSWAP! Heck, even Boms are on the Net. "On occasion," I said. "What do you want?"

"The question is: What do *you* want?"

"World peace. An end to hunger. A cool car," I said, trying not to pee in my pants. It's one thing to talk about aliens in the comfort of Mike's treehouse; it's another thing to be cross-examined by one.

"You are not amusing, Freakface. You asked for help."

"Not from you, I didn't," I said.

"We Boms believe in showing initiative." The creature's mouth twisted into a figure eight. I took a step back. Was it about to have me for supper? Then its translator box gurgled, and I realized it was chuckling. "I represent a party who is very interested in recovering your horned friend."

"You know about the Zephyr?" I asked.

"Now I do," the Bom said, its mouth turning inside out. My stomach lurched. A smiling Bom was not a pretty sight.

"I can't help you," I said.

"You may have no choice." The Bom burped.

"I don't know about your sewer of a planet. But this is the United States of America, of the planet Earth, and here I do have a choice. I'm not going to help you."

"You'll be sorry," the Bom said.

"What are you going to do? Sue me?"

The Bom's mouth straightened; the creature was no longer amused. "See you in court," it huffed. "By the way, I never lose."

It slimed up into the ceiling, leaving behind its stink—and a rotten feeling in my gut.

# 12

WHEN i RUSHED BACK OUT OF THE SHOWER
room to tell Jill about the Bom, I thought I was in
another world. The St. Mark's dining room was packed
with people of all sizes, shapes, ages, and smells.

There was a gang of old men in ragged caps and
heavy coats. "Old?" Quin said. "Sure, Jumpin' Joe is
seventy . . . but the Colonel, Gary, and Lou are all in
their forties."

"What happened to them?" I asked. Their hair
stuck up in wisps. The skin hung off their faces in
heavy folds.

"Life," Quin said. "It can wear a guy down."

A couple of men looked like any guys working in
a gas station or factory. One guy wore a white shirt
and tie. "They're struggling to get a new start," Quin
explained. "Come in mostly for meals."

"And them?" I asked, nodding at a group of young women, most of whom had babies or young children with them.

"Tough times at home," Quin said. "They need a safe place to stay, usually only for a few days while Social Services helps them find housing."

"How can there be so many?" I counted twenty-five adults and fourteen children. "Ashby is a small town."

"We serve the broader community," Quin said. "Some folks bus in for a good meal, then back to their jobs or rooms or whatever. Some stay the night." Quin turned me toward the food line. "Get yourself some chow. You've earned it."

Jill served me some lasagna from a big pan. Her hair, damp with sweat, curled under her hairnet. "Do you believe I have to wear this thing?" She snickered. "Just call me Queen Dork."

"Okay, your Royal Dweebness." I ducked as she tried to brain me with the spatula. I was about to tell her about the Bom when Ivy asked her to load the dishwasher.

I took my supper to an empty table in the corner and watched as Quin greeted people, calling them by name. He hugged a man with a scarred face as if he was his best friend. "How's the rash, Mr. Collins?" Quin asked.

The rash? I slid off my seat, checking for bugs and bacteria. I was still sneaking glances at my butt when I heard a *chomp-chomp*.

Burlap sat across the table from me, gulping down his salad like it was his first and only meal of the new millennium. His face was smeared with French dressing, his beard was dotted with bits of lettuce, and his hands—a spoon in each one—drove through the plate like a bulldozer.

He was the most beautiful sight I had ever seen.

"You came," I whispered. He glanced up, then pulled his tray closer to his chest.

"Hey, it's okay. I left you the note telling you about this place." I grabbed my tray and stood. "Before I get back to work, I have a question for you. You're . . . out on the street a lot. Have you seen anything . . . weird?"

Burlap ignored me as he swallowed a cherry tomato whole.

"A horse, running around. Maybe with something unusual on its head?"

Burlap glanced up at me. Even though his eyes were bloodshot and baggy, a spark of intelligence flickered within. For a moment, it was like he was looking right through me.

Judging me.

What gave a guy who bunked out on a grate the right to judge me? "Forget it," I snapped.

Burlap blinked, his eyes clouding up again. Then he grabbed what was left of my salad, put it on his tray, and hunkered down to finish his supper.

**69**

☆ ☆ ☆

When I went to tell Jill the good news, she had some of her own. "He's here," she said, her face glowing.

"I know. The guy shovels down chow like a garbage disposal. He's probably gnawing his way through the tray about now. He—"

Jill smacked me. "Why are you being so nasty? Are you jealous?"

"Why would I be jealous of Burlap?"

"Burlap?" Jill said. "Who's Bur— Oh yeah, that guy on the grate. You idiot, I'm not talking about him."

"So who are you talking about?" I asked.

Jill's eyes went gooey. "Troy," she said. "He's a volunteer here." I followed her lovesick stare across the room to where Troy was wiping tables. Wide shoulders, straight nose, good hair, cool clothes—Jill was right, the guy was bottom line awesome.

I hated him so much, I couldn't even breathe. "Don't you think it's a coincidence that he shows up here the same night we do?"

Jill grinned. "He must have found out I would be working here. So he volunteered, too."

"Oh, please. Last I looked, the world still revolved around the sun, not you."

"Well, why else would he be here?"

"New guy in town, new aliens in town. A coincidence?"

"'Oh, please' yourself. You're already obnoxious. Don't get paranoid on me." Jill gazed at Troy. "I think I'll go clear some tables."

"Time for scrubbing duty, Miss Pillsbury." Jill whipped around. Quin held up my scrub bucket, refurbished with a new bottle of disinfectant.

"But . . ." Jill sputtered. "I have kitchen duty."

"And you have performed it quite admirably." Quin pushed the bucket at her. "You were absolutely right—you Honor Society folks do know your duty. Don't you?"

"Yes sir," Jill said. She gave Troy one last look, then headed for the showers.

On top of being the handsomest dude this side of Jupiter, Troy was also the nicest.

"Let me help you with that," he said, reaching for the tray of dirty dishes.

"I got it," I mumbled, just as mountains of scraped lasagna avalanched off the plates and headed for my chest.

"No, you don't." Troy laughed, taking the tray from me.

We spent an hour scrubbing counters, loading the dishwasher, and scouring pans. Troy blabbered the whole time like he had known me forever, telling me how nice it was to move to Ashby and how cool the kids were.

"So, is that why you hang at St. Mark's?" I asked.

**71**

"To meet cool kids?"

"I'm new in town. Best way to get to know people is to volunteer somewhere."

"You want to get to know homeless people?"

"Let's just say—the best way to see how a place works is from the bottom up."

I grabbed a stack of clean plates from the dishwasher. As I was putting them away, I smelled something. "Hey, man," I said to Troy. "You been smoking?"

His movie star smile faded. "Of course not. You think I want to rot out my lungs?"

"Well, no offense or anything—but you're reeking of the stuff."

"When I took the trash out, a bunch of the clients were passing a cigar around in the back parking lot. I must have picked it up on my clothes. Bummer, huh?" Troy winked, then went back to the dishwasher.

Bummer. Especially since the Dumpster was in the side alley, not the back parking lot.

# 13

I CAME OUT OF THE KITCHEN AND GOT
lost in a maze.

"Wh-what the heck?" I stuttered as I walked into
a wall that hadn't been there thirty minutes ago.

"Room dividers," Ivy said. "We have the big room
for meals, then we pull out the dividers and create
smaller rooms for support groups."

"Support groups? For what?"

"Tonight we have a pediatric nurse working with
the young mothers, talking about immunizations
and proper nutrition," Ivy explained. "Alcoholics
Anonymous is running a meeting. And we have
someone from the state housing authority helping
people fill out applications for permanent housing."

Permanent housing. It would be nice if Burlap
would find his way into that meeting.

"The AA meeting is closed to volunteers, but feel free to peek into the other groups," Ivy said.

The young women were talking about diaper rash; the older women were talking about quitting smoking. The door to the AA meeting was closed, but I heard roars of laughter coming through the fabric walls. Life may not always be so nice, but hey, die laughing.

I couldn't find Burlap anywhere. Maybe he only came for supper. Maybe he didn't realize he could sleep here, too. Maybe no one had ever told him he could freeze to death on a night like this.

I grabbed the last two bags of trash and my coat, telling Ivy that I was going out to the Dumpster.

"Don't fall in," she said with a laugh.

If only that was the worst that could happen.

The street in front of the church was quiet; the side alley was empty. Where had Burlap gone? And why was I out here in the dark, looking for him? Sure, the guy had problems. No place to live, raggedy clothes, and no table manners. But I had aliens and time warps and foulmouthed Draconians on my tail. And then there was the Bom, threatening to take me to court. So if Burlap didn't care about himself, why should I do the work for him?

I dragged the trash bags out to the Dumpster and flung them in.

"Ooof."

*Ooof*? What rat says *ooof*? I knew I should turn tail and run.

Instead, I hoisted myself up and looked in. Soggy newspapers, paper plates, and industrial-size food containers floated in a sea of trash bags. The thing stunk, but not of Bom or smoke—just of pure, all-American trash.

The bags shifted. I backed away. Anything emerging from a Dumpster was bound to have a bad attitude. Another bag moved, and a head appeared. Knitted hat, flapped cap, ragged kerchief.

Burlap. His beard hung with bits of wet paper and ripped plastic.

"You!" I said. "What're you doing in there?"

His eyes were dull and confused, as if he didn't *know* what he was doing there. I felt sick, a deeper sick than I had ever felt before, except when Dad told me he and Mom were splitting up. The kind of sick that worms into your gut and never goes away. Burlap didn't have a clue how he had gotten into the Dumpster, and he didn't know where he should go next. He was a soul so pathetic he couldn't tell a trash heap from a hot-air grate from a warm cot.

"Come on." I put out my hand. "Let's get you out of there." Burlap froze. His eyes cleared, like the clouds parting at night to show a full moon. "What?" I said. Then I heard what.

Hoofbeats.

*Oh no. Not here, not now. I'm in too much trouble*

*already.* I jumped onto the top of the Dumpster. "Go back!" I shouted. "I can't deal with you tonight!"

There was a rustling behind me. I turned in time to see Burlap lumbering down the alley, toward the back of St. Mark's.

I jumped down and raced in the opposite direction. The street was clear of horses, though a few cars passed. I listened; the hoofbeats had disappeared. Maybe I had just imagined them. Maybe the *pum-pum* had come from a fat jogger pounding down the sidewalk or some heavy bass line in someone's CD player.

*I should just go back inside.* I shivered; ice crystals danced on the night wind. *No one should be out on a night like this.*

I sighed and headed back down the alley.

The parking lot held a few cars, probably belonging to the social workers and volunteers. A white van was parked near the back door. "St. Mark's Shelter" was painted in blue on its side.

Suddenly the parking lot was drowned in darkness. Vast shadows drifted overhead, blocking the sky and the moon—shadows with wings and streams of smoke.

Frigid air buffeted me as wings flapped wildly all around me. I raced across the lot and rolled under the van to hide. As I lay there panting, the light came back.

The shadows shifted again toward the back fence, moving like a cloud of black locusts. There had to be ten of the huge LizardPukes, but they moved as one, swirling like a cyclone. As their shadows intertwined and the spiral tightened, I realized they were taking aim at their prey.

Burlap.

He was huddled on the ground, his head between his legs, quivering like a rag-covered jellyfish.

The spiral whipped sideways, preparing to strike.

Two quick rolls from under the van to the back door and I'd be inside, safe. Lots of fire extinguishers and a sprinkler system and showers in there. And big Quin would do anything to protect his clients.

But Burlap was *my* client.

The spiral of beasts was almost on him now. I rolled out from under the van and looked frantically for a weapon. There's never a laser cannon in a church parking lot when you need one.

I jumped into the van. The parking lot sloped downhill from the back door to a high chain-link fence. I yanked off the emergency brake, slammed the shift into neutral, jumped out, and started pushing.

The spiral was inches away from Burlap's head now, a giant whip ready to strike. There were no flames yet, only smoke and that crackling noise that meant the beasts were about to hawk up fireballs.

The van began to move. I jumped in and grabbed the steering wheel, turning it toward Burlap. The van picked up speed. I leaned on the horn.

The spiral split apart. There was a burst of flames, and a ring of fire exploded around Burlap. He just huddled in the middle as if it would all go away if he didn't look up, didn't move.

The night was black with wings and white with flames.

The van rolled faster. I pounded on the horn. "Get in!" I yelled. "Or get out of the stupid way, at least!"

Burlap's coverings caught fire, like straw bursting into flames. I jumped out of the van and pushed him to the ground, rolling him to smother the flames.

CRASH! The van hit the back fence. I couldn't look, because now that I had gotten Burlap rolling, he kept going. He was inches away from the ring of fire. I had to jump over him and shove him in the opposite direction.

"Idiot," I yelled. "Do something to help yourself!"

Something grabbed me from behind. I whipped around, kicking and punching.

"What's going on here?" Quin growled. He held me with steel arms, and I realized that under all the Kris Kringle cheer there was some serious muscle.

"The fire!" I panted, and indeed, there was fire

everywhere. The dried bushes and broken-down fence blazed. Even the van smoldered; some of the sparks must have spread to the interior.

Ivy and Dana Pillsbury were going nuts, spraying fire extinguishers everywhere. In the distance, sirens wailed. Someone had called the fire department.

Quin wouldn't let me go. "Who started this fire?" he said, his voice hard in my ear.

"Why . . ." I gasped. What could I say? Aliens attacked Burlap and I came to his rescue?

"That man started it. The one with the heavy beard."

I whirled and saw Troy standing there, his arm around Jill. He nodded at me, his eyes heavy with concern and sympathy.

"What . . . what did you say?" I asked.

"I was in the kitchen, cleaning the exhaust hood. I glanced out the window. Something was burning," Troy continued. "I ran out and saw that man, the one with the funny clothes, trying to keep warm by a fire in a trash can. But he spooked and tipped it, and it spread on the ground. I came back inside to get an extinguisher, not realizing it would spread so rapidly."

Quin's hands relaxed on my arm. He was buying Troy's story.

"When I saw Nick trying to chase the guy away, that's when I ran in to get you, Quin," Troy concluded. Jill smiled up at Troy as if he was the only sun in her orbit.

Quin grabbed me tightly again, this time in a hug. "I'm glad you're okay, Nick," he whispered. "But next time a situation comes up, come get me or Ivy. Okay?"

"Any situation?" I whispered.

"Of course," he said with a laugh. "You just come to me. No questions asked."

Nice man, Quin. But he didn't have a clue.

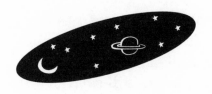

# 14

"HE **LiED**," i **SAiD.**

"He did it to save your butt," Jill said, still starry-eyed. When Dana had driven Troy home last night, Mr. Perfection had kissed her good-bye.

That smoke-sucking son-of-a-Loapher.

The next morning was Saturday. Dana and Pam Pillsbury had wanted to take us all out for breakfast but we begged off. Jill, Mike, and I needed the time alone to talk.

"I don't trust that Troy," I growled.

"You're jealous." Jill laughed.

I blushed, then dropped my bagel on the floor to hide my red face. "Jealous of that guy?" I said from under the table. "What's he got that I don't?"

Jill smiled dreamily. "Well, since you asked, let's see . . . should I start with his hair or his shoulders?

**81**

His eyes, that's it."

Mike mock-barfed his orange juice. "Do you mind not gushing while I'm trying to eat?"

"Shut up, Albert," Jill said.

"You shut up," he snapped back. "We've got out-of-control aliens setting half the town on fire, and all you can think about is your infantile little life and your infantile little crush."

Jill stormed out of the kitchen.

"Where do you think you're going?" Mike yelled.

"To brush my infantile little teeth, you infantile little jerk," she shrieked from the hall.

"Great." Mike gave me a dirty look. "See what you did?"

"Me? I was just minding my own business," I said.

"Open mouth, insert foot," Mike said.

"Open Earth, insert alien," I said with a sigh.

Jill stood on her bed, shrieking her brains out. In the middle of her floor sat the biggest, ugliest rat I had ever seen.

"Kill it!" Jill screamed.

"Shut that thing up!" the rat screamed back.

"You came!" I shouted.

"What did you say?" she yelled.

"You came," I said.

But Jill was looking at the rat. "Wh-a-a-t?" she stammered.

"I told you to shut up," it growled.

Jill's eyes rolled skyward. I caught her before she hit the floor. The rat thing sniffed as it watched me staggering around with Jill in my arms.

"I can see why you need help," it said. "You're quite pathetic."

*And you're butt ugly*, I wanted to say. But you don't look a gift rat in the mouth.

"You called for help?" Mike said to me.

"You told me to, right?" I answered.

"Yeah, but . . ." We both stared. The rat thing was the color of cardboard and the size of a scrawny cat. It had pointy ears, bugged-out eyes, and a wet nose.

"A Chihuahua," Jill murmured as she came to. "I thought it was a talking rat. . . ."

The rat thing raised its whiskery brows at us. "I've been called some foul things before," it said, "but never a rodent. Or a Chilly-wawa."

"Chihuahua," Mike said. He automatically corrects anyone who is wrong.

"Whatever. My name is Titan. I am a Sirian, and proud of it."

"But you don't look anything like Barnabus. Or Ditka," Mike said.

"Overgrown louts, the lot of them. Substituting muscle for brainpower." Titan sniffed. "Which one of you is Freakface?"

Jill smacked me. "I should have known."

No, I should have known. Just my luck—I ask for

a hero and I get an overgrown rodent. Who is *proud of it*, no less.


It was the filthiest word in Mike Pillsbury's vocabulary.

"Wrong?" he yelled. "I'm *wrong*?"

"Right. You are wrong," Titan said, his voice from the translator box sounding like a chipmunk squeak.

"I'm never wrong!" Mike yelled. "Never!"

Jill and I looked at each other, then started laughing our butts off. "No? What about the time you used superglue as toothpaste, thinking you'd never have to brush your teeth again?" Jill laughed. "You had tooth trash stuck to your molars for months!"

"I was four years old!"

"And what about the time . . . when was it?" I crinkled my face, pretending to think hard. "Oh yeah. Last week! When you tried to hook my television up to your satellite dish and you blew it up, and now I have to watch black-and-white television!"

"I said I was sorry!" Mike cried. "Anyway, that's different. This is a Chronicle we're talking about."

"Oh, really?" I said. "What about the Chronicle when the Garbage Cans took over Town Hall and trashed it?"

"I was five years old when I made that one up!" Mike wailed. "But these days . . ." Mike's face darkened. "Since the Hanzels, the Jong, the Lyra . . . I haven't been wrong."

"Well, you're wrong now," Titan squeaked. "No, I take that back, you are right about one thing. Zephyrs are the most stubborn beasts in the universe. But you're wrong about the most important thing."

"What's that?" I asked.

"Zephyrs are not people."

"Neither are you," Jill said. "You're a talking rat."

"Jill, listen. The universe is filled with people who don't look like us, act like us, even think like us," Mike explained, playing professor. "The Xgonearks are fire-breathing rocks, but they're as much people as we are. The Mantix—curse their sorry souls—are mud-covered lumps, but they're people."

"And what qualifies these rat freaks of yours to be called people?" Jill asked.

"Intelligence," Titan said.

"And moral sense," Mike added. "A *person* makes a choice for right or wrong. An animal or plant just doesn't know any better."

"So what about the Zephyrs?" I asked. "In Mike's Chronicle they're intelligent, but they choose not to be civilized."

Titan sniffed. "In real life they are no smarter than your average Earth cow. But unfortunately, they're tremendously dangerous."

"How?" I asked. "They don't breathe fire, do they?"

"Good grief, no," Titan said. "But they consume grass and trees like your locusts do, killing continents at a time. And worse, when panicked, they stampede. They killed a hundred Draconians—"

"I knew it!" Mike said. "That was part of the Chronicle!"

"*Unarmed* Draconians, who simply wanted to try to breed the bad attitude out of these beasts so they could be useful. But it is no use. The Zephyrs are a danger to any thinking race they come into contact with. No race will offer them sanctuary because they ruin ecosystems. The Council has decreed that these animals—"

"You mean these people!" I argued.

"I said what I meant. Animals." Titan glared. "They are dumb, dangerous beasts that the Council has decided must be neutralized."

"You have no right to kill harmless creatures!" Jill said.

"No, we don't. But we have a responsibility to contain dangerous, violent beasts," Titan replied. "Even if it means destroying them."

"And you call yourself civilized?" Jill said. "Nick says the Zephyr is beautiful!"

"You call yourself intelligent?" Titan sniffed. "You

**86**

who judge by outward beauty and not by inward worth?"

*Judging*. There had been something clear and true and terrible in the way the Zephyr had stared me down with his silver eyes that could see beyond today.

Something intelligent.

"You're wrong!" I yelled. "You can't destroy the Zephyrs! They're people, too."

Mike sighed. Suddenly he seemed defeated. "You saw one Zephyr . . . once. So how can you know?"

"I just know!" I said.

"How could you possibly know that?" Titan snapped.

"I don't know! Maybe I got it straight from the horse's mouth!" I said.

"And Nick's going to prove it!" Jill said.

"How?" Titan asked.

"Tell them how, Nick!" Jill said. Her eyes were bright, as if she actually believed I could do something to save the horned horse.

"I'm going to catch the Zephyr and ride him," I said with great certainty. Inside, my guts turned to water.

"Zephyrs bend their backs to no one," Titan said.

"So I've been told." I laughed. "But maybe I can persuade this Zephyr—"

Titan laughed like a cat coughing up a hairball.

"And that will prove the Zephyr's intelligence? Letting a Freakface ride him?"

It was Mike's turn to laugh. "Hey, Nick. It took a visitor from outer space, but you've been roasted good."

I had a thousand comebacks, but for once I kept my mouth shut. Sure, I had been roasted. But not by any mangy Sirian and his lame jokes.

I had been roasted by a fire-breathing, flying LizardPuke who had the hots for my Zephyr. And I was determined to get to the Zephyr before he got roasted, too.

# 15

"THIS IS VERY FOOLISH," TITAN GROWLED.

"Hear that, Mike?" I laughed, pulling up the hood of my jacket. "My reputation has preceded me clear across the galaxy."

"If Titan is right, you can't catch the Zephyr anyway," Mike warned. "But by luring him, you could be endangering the neighborhood. Maybe the whole town. The whole state. The whole—"

"Shut up, Albert," Jill said. "You think you're so smart."

"He *is* so smart," I said. "Which is why I believe him over Mighty Mouse here."

Titan showed his teeth. "Sometimes civilization is overrated. Sometimes a hard bite to the posterior is the best recourse. Sometimes—"

Mike stepped between the Sirian and my butt.

"I'm smart enough to know we can trust Titan."

"What? Sirians never make mistakes?" I asked.

"Never!" Titan's pint-sized growl sounded like a hair dryer.

"Besides, we promised my parents we'd stay in," Mike said. "You and Jill are on probation."

"Everyone knows you can't believe a word I say," I snapped. "So—are you *in* or are you *out*?"

Mike stood silent, his arms folded over his chest. Titan sat at his side, looking equally stubborn.

I dragged Mike into the living room, out of Titan's earshot. "You promised we'd stick together, no matter what."

"You're the one breaking the promise, Nick. Trying to catch a dangerous beast."

"He's not dangerous," I snapped.

"Titan says he is," Mike said. "I'm sorry, Nick. No one wants to see an innocent creature harmed. But I have to believe what Titan says."

"And that's the real problem, isn't it?" I said. "You're always throwing me off for someone better. Katelyn. Schreiber. And now this loudmouthed rat."

"That loudmouthed rat is a highly respected, well-traveled, intergalactic relief worker—"

"And I'm a total loser. So I'll go off and do what losers do." I stormed out of the living room, almost trampling Titan. As I opened the front door, I turned to say good-bye to Jill.

She was dressed for cold weather, so cute in her

ski coat, knit hat, and fuzzy mittens that I could barely breathe.

"What're you doing?" I gasped.

She glared at Mike. "Tell Mom and Dad we've gone for a walk. Right, Nick?"

"Um . . . right," I said.

"Wrong!" Mike yelped. As I slammed the door on his protests, I felt like I was slamming the door on my life. Mike had been my friend forever, there for all the tough times, even when Dad walked out on us. And now I was walking out on him.

But I was walking out with Jill, so somehow I didn't feel so lost.

"What's the plan?" Jill asked. I shivered inside my coat. It was below freezing, and the wind whipped hard through the bare trees.

"Plan?" I mumbled. What *was* my plan? That was Mike's job; I had assumed he would be part of this. As I pondered the matter, I didn't see the ice slick; I slipped and went down hard. "Yow!"

"Walk much?" Jill laughed as she helped me up.

"Jeepers, it's not even Christmas yet and—I've got it!" I shouted.

"Got what?"

"Titan said the Zephyrs consume vegetation like locusts. Look around you, Jill."

The neighborhood was white. The hedges, trees, and bushes had lost their leaves a month ago and the evergreens were iced up. The only green was in the wreaths on doors.

"It snowed three days ago, then it all iced up," I reasoned. "He's got to be starving."

"You told me he runs fast," Jill said. "He's probably in California or Florida right now, munching on palm trees."

"I don't think so," I said. "There must be something he needs here, which is why he's hanging around."

"So the plan is . . ." Jill said.

"We set a banquet table." I grinned. "Then wait for our guest of honor to show up."

We were all baited up, with no place to go.

"Now what?" Jill cried. "I'm freezing, and so is the lettuce."

When we had realized we weren't going to find any grass or leaves this time of year, we had raided my refrigerator. Mom was on another diet and ate three meals a day of green stuff I couldn't even name, let alone stomach.

"Spinach, broccoli, romaine, endive, leeks, watercress," Jill listed.

"How do you know all this?" I asked. "You live on tacos and fries."

"For future reference," Jill said. "Just in case my hips ever catch up to my appetite."

We loaded up two shopping bags, then walked around the block, trying to figure out what to do next. I silently cursed Mike for bailing on us. Jill might be an honor student, but Mike was the creative genius we needed.

"Now what?" Jill said again, this time whacking me.

"What, abuse is going to make me think faster? Okay, let me put on my geek hat and pretend I'm Mike. Use logic and reason. Twice I went into a time warp in school; the other time I was in Mike's treehouse. And that time, I heard hoofbeats from the back woods. So what connects these places?"

"The access road in the woods behind our yards!" Jill exclaimed. "It cuts under the high-power wires, behind the town center, and then by the middle school. Hey! And it ends at the transformer station behind the mall."

"So let's assume the Zephyr is running that path," I said. "We can lay out the stuff there. Where are we going to lure him?"

"How about your garage?"

"If he makes a lot of noise or kicks out the walls, my mother will freak," I said. "Ever since my father left, she sleeps with my baseball bat under her bed, convinced burglars are going to get us."

We walked some more, lost in thought. The sharp ice and biting cold made the shining holiday lights seem like a cruel joke. There were lots of cars out. This was Saturday; Christmas was Tuesday, so there were only a couple of shopping days left. But all the skaters and sliders had enough sense to stay in.

"Nick, this is stupid." Jill grabbed my arm. "We don't know what we're doing. Let's go back."

I pulled away. "No. I have this gut feeling that these people—the Sirians and Draconians and Boms and Mike—they just don't *get* the Zephyr."

"Like people don't get you, Nick?" Jill's voice was so gentle, my throat twisted with that funny feeling you get when you're trying hard not to cry.

"Maybe," I said.

"Okay," Jill said. "Then I think I have an idea."

We started the trail of goodies in the woods behind the Pillsburys' backyard.

"Not too much," Jill warned. "Just enough to whet the Zephyr's appetite. We want him to have to follow the trail all the way to the courts. We'll grab him there."

The access road ran between the school building and the playing fields, including the football, soccer, and softball fields. Far back, there were community tennis courts, bounded by high chain-link fencing and shielded from the school grounds by a row of evergreens.

"No one comes here this time of year. The fence is fifteen feet high, and we can lock the court," Jill said. She had brought a bicycle lock to secure the gate. Our bait trail ended inside the tennis courts

**94**

with a pile of red cabbage and green lettuce.

"So, now what?" I said, sitting on the time-keeper's bench. "We just wait?"

"I suppose," Jill said. She checked her watch. "It's after four. My parents will be home from shopping by six. What about your mom?"

"She's working second shift at the hospital tonight, so I'm spending the night at your house."

We huddled on the bench, watching clouds race across the gray sky. Jill shivered and pushed against me, trying to keep warm. I held my breath and hoped the moment would last forever.

Minutes passed. Then more minutes. I glanced at my watch; it was 4:56. Darkness was falling; December days were the shortest of the year.

"There's got to be more than the access road that draws the Zephyr," I said through chattering teeth.

"Of course," Jill said. "Why didn't I think of that? It's *you*. You're the common denominator. What do you do that makes him come your way?"

"Maybe he likes my sick jokes," I said with a laugh.

"No one likes your sick jokes," Jill said. "Come on, Nick. Think. There must be something you did that somehow involved you with him. What were you doing each time?"

"The first time I was making fun of Fleming. The second time I was daydreaming. The last time . . . I was with you in the tutoring center."

"And what were you thinking?" Jill asked.

What was I thinking? That Fleming was about to take my head off; that I was losing Mike's friendship; that Jill was rattling on about Troy.

"Nothing special," I said. "Except that I would rather be somewhere else than where I was."

"That's it!" Jill said, jumping up. "The Zephyr would relate to that, with all his running around. Do it now."

"I don't think I can think on demand," I said.

Jill sat down and put her arm around me. "Come on, Nick," she whispered. "Think about being someplace really cool."

Cool? Actually, I was already contemplating someplace hot. A beach with white sand and crystal-clear water. Bright but not burning sun, more of a quiet warmth. A breeze, with the smell of pineapples and oranges and a dash of Jill.

What was Jill doing in my daydream, with her hair shining in the sun, her feet dancing in the waves?

I walked toward the water, feeling the sun on my back, the hot sand between my toes. My feet crunched on the sand. Jill spotted me now and waved, her smile outshining the sun.

I walked faster, my footsteps now *plum-plum-plum* in the sand.

I suddenly realized that the *plum-plum-plum*

was outside my head, coming down the trail. These were not hoofbeats, but footsteps, tromping in the wet snow.

An uninvited guest was heading our way.

# 16

PLUM-CHOMP, PLUM-CHOMP. BURLAP stumbled along our bait trail, stuffing his face on half-frozen watercress.

"What are you doing here?" Jill scolded. "I thought you learned your lesson."

Burlap glanced dimly at her, then settled back to his greens grubbing.

"You idiot," I cursed. "You good-for-nothing, useless . . ." I wanted to kick his sorry butt to St. Mark's and back. Burlap jerked his arms up and covered his head as if he could read my mind.

"Stop it," Jill hissed. "You're scaring him."

"He needs to be scared! He almost got fried last night. But is he doing anything about it? Oh, no. Instead, he's under our feet again, messing up our plan."

Jill sighed. "This was a waste of time. He probably ate all our bait. We might as well go home."

"Fine," I said. We turned around and started walking. We were almost back to the tennis courts when we stopped and looked at each other.

"He'll freeze," Jill said.

"He deserves to," I snapped.

"You don't mean that," she said.

"Yes. I do." Then I sighed. "But what the heck, I'm hanging out with an Honor Society member. So let's go do your duty and retrieve the guy."

We were halfway down the road again when we heard the *tum-tum-tum*, rapidly growing into a *pound-pound-pound*. Jill and I looked at each other again.

"Hoofbeats," she whispered.

*This is what we wanted,* I thought as we disappeared in a flash of light.

We landed with a *thud* in the tennis courts. While I was still digging my head out of the net, Jill had raced to the gate, slammed it shut, and locked it.

"What happened?" I moaned. "Are we in the time warp?"

"We did it!" Jill pointed skyward. "Look!" Clouds drifted across the moon. An icy breeze rustled the dry bushes. Somehow, we had managed to dodge the time warp and stay in real time. I *felt* the cold.

Then I felt the fury of the Zephyr as he

charged across the court.

"Run!" I yelled. Jill was already scaling the fence when I caught up with her. We had gotten ten feet up when the Zephyr reached us, bucking and kicking the chain link.

"Hold on!" I yelled to Jill.

Jill was still climbing. My lungs were bursting. How did a Homecoming Princess get to be such a monkey? Between rammings, I crept upward until I finally joined her at the top.

Jill radiated victory. "That little rat said we couldn't do it. But we did! We caught the Zephyr."

Indeed, the creature was pacing the courts, nosing the fence for a way out. Even in the moonlight, he threw off his own glow, shifting tones of silver and red.

"How did we escape the time warp?" I panted.

"I'm guessing the fence did it," Jill said. "Assuming the Zephyr drags us into the time warp with him, we must have stopped his forward momentum by trapping him in the courts."

"You sound just like your brother," I said.

Jill whacked me.

"Hey, that was a compliment!" I cried. "Now what do we do?"

"I thought you had a plan."

"To catch him. Not to keep him," I said. "I know one thing—we can't tell Mike. He'll tell the Sirian."

"Oh no." Jill groaned.

"What?"

She pointed. Below us, the Zephyr was getting ready to charge something huddled in the corner of the court.

Burlap.

"He must have gotten swept in with us," Jill said. We slid back down the fence.

"Hey, you!" I shouted as the Zephyr rose on his hind legs, about to pound Burlap's lights out.

The Zephyr turned to me. The light in his eyes was as sharp as steel.

"Remember me?" I grinned. "We're supposed to be—"

The Zephyr lowered his head and charged. "Buddies!" I screamed, as I tumbled over the net.

The Zephyr leaped over it easily. I tripped, ending up under the creature's hooves, remembering Titan's warning that Zephyrs stampede when panicked. I saw my life passing before me—Mom and Dad and Mike—and I felt sick when I couldn't even remember my half sisters' names.

"Stop that!" Jill yelled.

The Zephyr froze, as if suddenly cast into its own time warp.

"We're here to help you," Jill continued, her voice softer. The Zephyr turned. Jill and the creature locked eyes in a stare as electric as a wire.

Jill smiled. The creature blinked. Jill motioned with her mittened hand, then turned her back and

**101**

headed for the bench. I wanted to cry *No! Don't you know how sharp that horn is?* But she walked so calmly, I had to pray she knew what she was doing.

The Zephyr followed her. Jill sat down on the bench and the creature towered over her, a bundle of power.

Jill took off her mitten and reached for the Zephyr's nose.

The creature who bends his back to no one bowed to Jill.

She smiled as she stroked his face. A silver hush fell over all of us; even Burlap straightened out of his own mess and stared, his eyes at least clear, if not comprehending.

*Peace on Earth and goodwill to men,* I thought. *Maybe we can pull it off.*

I smelled him before I saw him.

"Bom!" I hissed.

The gate to the courts, still secured with Jill's bike lock, burst open with a flash and a *whack.*

"Gross," Jill squealed as the Bom slimed his way onto the tennis courts. The Zephyr reared; Jill quieted him with a touch. Burlap sat in the corner and rocked quietly, oblivious to everything except the head of lettuce he nibbled.

"What do you want, you sack of scum?" I said.

"I'm here to claim what rightfully belongs to my client," the Bom said. "Surrender the beast."

"Bayurd is not going anywhere," Jill said. She blinked hard; her eyes watered from the odor.

"Who is Bayurd?" I hissed.

"The Zephyr," she hissed back.

How did she know that? The Zephyr hadn't spoken a word. If Titan was right, he *couldn't* speak.

"You heard the lady," I said. "Barnyard—"

"Bayurd," Jill snapped. Pillsburys automatically correct anyone who is wrong.

"Bayurd stays with us," I said.

"I have a Federation order for removal of the Zephyr into my custody!" the Bom stormed. His orifices exuded steam; the smell whacked us like a wall of rotting seaweed.

"Tough." I gagged. "This is Earth. We're not *allowed* to belong to your stinking Federation, remember? So you can take that order for removal and stuff it where the stars don't shine."

The Bom harumphed from every orifice. Gas popped from him like a thousand balloons. A green haze filled the courts. Jill kept her hand on the Zephyr's face, steadying him. The creature's nostrils flared, then closed tight.

The Bom's mouth twisted into a pretzel.

"What's that GasBag doing?" Jill said.

"Attorney PusPocket is laughing," I said.

"Laughing? What's so funny?" Jill asked.

My stomach sank like a lead weight. "Nothing to us," I answered. "But the Bom, apparently, finds our

**103**

situation hilarious."

"Situation? What situ—" Jill paled as her eyes followed mine upward. Perched above us, like gargoyles ready to spring, were ten LizardPukes.

Leaking smoke and ready to fire.

# 17

"IT'S WRONG!" JILL CRIED.

"What does the law have to with right or wrong?" the Bom humphed. "It's simply a question of what must be. The courts have ordered this Zephyr to be delivered to my client's custody. Dead or alive."

The creature was strangely calm, standing by Jill's side while the Bom and I debated his fate.

"And who exactly is your client?" I asked.

"That is none of your business," the Bom fumed.

"It's those Draconians, isn't it?" I said. "They want to kill our Zephyr."

"They have the legal right to do whatever they please," the Bom replied. "Now, release the creature to me."

"No!" Jill and I shouted in unison.

We were at a standoff. Some standoff—the Bom

had Federation law and an army of smoking vultures. I had my belief that the Zephyr was more than he seemed. But I didn't have much else. I didn't have Mike Pillsbury's brainpower or Scott Schreiber's mighty muscles. What weapon did I have to match the firepower lined up against us?

Then I realized—call it a blessing or a curse—that I had the absolute inability to keep my mouth shut. And I knew more about ducking and running than anyone on Earth. Maybe even beyond.

The LizardPukes—I refused to dignify them by calling them Draconians—towered over us, their jaws smoking, their translator boxes glistening around their necks. Translator boxes meant they could understand every word we spoke.

I glanced at Jill and mouthed *Trust me*. She crossed her eyes in disbelief. Then she tightened her grip on the Zephyr's mane, bit her lower lip, and nodded.

I raised my fists in my best Schreiber imitation. "Wanna fight?" I growled, looking up at the Bom's smoking army. The line of LizardPukes rippled and hissed but they held their formation.

"Hey! I'm talking to you up there!" I rattled the fence. "You come down here, you chicken poops!"

The beasts' mighty wings blocked out the moonlight as they spiraled down to the courts and reassembled behind the Bom.

**106**

"They are down here," said the Bom. "As you requested."

*Now would be a good time to take it back, Thorpe,* I told myself.

Instead, I swaggered up to the biggest beast and waved my fist under his snout. "Come on, put 'em up," I challenged. He turned his massive head toward the Bom.

The Bom pointed a tentacle at me. "This puny human is not likely to be a threat," he humphed. "But just in case . . ."

The LizardPukes circled me, leaving Jill and the Zephyr unguarded.

*Gotcha,* I thought.

*Now don't get me,* I prayed.

I stepped up to the biggest beast again. Its eyes glowed green and mean. "Hey, what's that strange tumor on your neck?" I shouted. "Oh, sorry. It's your head!"

I doubled over with fake laughter, all the time watching the beast's eyes. They blinked, then narrowed as it comprehended the insult.

I did a one-eighty and walked to the beast immediately across from Green Eyes. His scales were a crusty brown. "Are you always this ugly, or is today a special occasion?" I taunted. Crusty jerked back in surprise. Flames flickered between his scruffy lips.

"I would not antagonize my troops, Freakface,"

**107**

the Bom warned. "They have little tolerance for insults."

"Too bad," I snapped. "I'm just getting warmed up." As I turned back to Green Eyes, I stared at Jill. "Get ready to boogie," I whispered.

"Boogie? What's Boogie?" the Bom asked, suspicious.

I stood on my tiptoes, barely reaching the crest of what I assumed was Green Eye's chest. "Did I say boogie? I mean boogers—what this birdbrain is full of," I said. "But maybe your translator doesn't recognize it. Perhaps the term 'snot' would be more meaningful?"

"*Th*not?" Green Eyes growled, speaking for the first time. I doubled with laughter, genuine this time.

"Snot," I said, trying to imitate Mike's professor's voice. "That gooey, green gunk that forms in your nose when you're so full of disgusting slime that it backs up through your whole body and worms its way out through those putrid stinkholes you call nostrils."

"You whimpering piece of human rubbish," Green Eyes sneered. "I should—"

"What are you mad at me for?" I asked, trying to relax my face into little-kid innocence. "He . . ." I nodded behind me at Crusty. "He's the one who said your boogers couldn't light a candle to his."

Green Eyes glared over my head at Crusty.

Crusty glared back, smoke leaking from his eyelids. Yep, the fuel was on the fire. Now to strike the match.

I trotted back to Crusty. "You know what he said about you?"

"That fool is always insulting me," Crusty snarled in a voice like rusty nails. "What did he say this time?"

I leaned in close, playing conspirator. "He said you were a . . ." I gasped. "I can't repeat it. It's too awful."

Crusty glared over my head at Green Eyes. "Tell me!" he shrieked, spitting sparks.

I motioned him closer to me. "He said you were . . . oh, it's so cruel!"

"What!" the creature yowled.

"He said you were . . . a . . . a nonsmoker!"

"A nonsmoker!" Crusty reared back his ugly head and hawked out a glob of fire. I hit the ground, my butt sizzling as Crusty's flame passed over me and nailed Green Eyes. The big beast roared, then hammered back a fireball as big as a watermelon.

With fire erupting everywhere, the LizardPukes went wild, throwing flames at each other and anything that moved.

Through the rising inferno, I saw Jill and the Zephyr slip away. The Bom, keeping his eye on business, saw me creeping after them. But every time he burped a warning, it burst into flames.

I crawled, scurried, and slinked my way to the gate, ready to escape into the dark. Then I tripped over something. Burlap. He was curled into a tight ball, trembling with fear. I yanked him up. "Come on!"

The chain-link fence melted in sizzling globs around us as we pushed through the gate. We stumbled down the access road, where I hoped Jill and the Zephyr would be waiting for us. Was anything else waiting for us?

Was I jumping out of the fire only to find myself in the frying pan?

After depositing Burlap back at St. Mark's, Jill and I raced home, using the access road to hide the Zephyr from the rest of Ashby. I ran into the Pillsburys' house, sweat frozen in clumps on my hood and my coat putrid with smoke. Mike and Titan never gave me a glance. They just assumed that we would fail in our quest.

Just as they assumed they would succeed.

"It's really the only right thing to do," Mike said apologetically as he and Titan demonstrated a bizarre electronic device sitting in the middle of the Pillsburys' living room.

"Michael Pillsbury is everything that our legends say," Titan gushed like a buzzing mosquito. "Clever, imaginative, inventive."

I stifled a yawn as Mike droned on about his and the Sirian's invention. The bait was radicchio—

expensive red lettuce. The signal was designed to lure the Zephyr. The halter would snap around the Zephyr's muzzle when he bent down to feed. A gentle tranquilizer would be injected into the creature's neck and put him to sleep.

"You're not killing my Zephyr!" I yelled.

"I'm just making him sleepy!" Mike yelled back.

I glared at Titan. "Right. Let someone else do the dirty work."

"Anyway," Mike said, "the device has a detection alarm to alert us if the Zephyr comes within a mile of this house." Mike pointed to a light on the device, then to the electronic bracelet that he wore on his wrist. Titan wore a similar module on his translator collar. "When this light flashes red, we'll know the Zephyr is approaching."

Something moved in the hall. I held my breath. As planned, Jill and the Zephyr crept quietly up the stairs, a mere whisper compared to Mike's snooze-inducing lecture. When Jill and Bayurd disappeared from sight, I exhaled softly, trying to suppress a snort of laughter.

Mike's red light never blinked once.

# 18

THE ZEPHYR ALARM WENT OFF AT 1 A.M.

I tumbled out of the top bunk and landed on Mike's head. Mike stumbled around like a blind man, feeling his desk and bureau for his glasses. I had hidden them earlier on his top bookshelf in case I needed to make a fast getaway.

"Let's go get him!" Titan yipped.

"Wait!" I said. "You don't want to alert Mike's parents. Let me go outside and check the device while Mike finds his specs."

"You can't be trusted!" Titan said, nipping at my heels.

"You're right," I mumbled as I closed the door on Titan's ugly little snout.

I fumbled down the hall. The Pillsbury house was my second home, so I didn't need the light.

What would I find in Mike's trap? Before Mike and I had sacked out for the night, Jill had whispered that the Zephyr was sleeping in her room, satisfied with the seven salads she had ordered to go with our pizzas.

But if not the Zephyr, then what?

I stepped into the frigid night. The moon had set; the only light was from the Pillsburys' back porch and the blinking of the red warning light. Mike and Titan had moved their device to beyond the elm tree. A rounded shape took form over it. A big dog? A small bear? A new alien?

*Chomping.*

"You goofball!" I said. "We took you to the shelter. Why did you leave?"

Burlap munched the radicchio Mike had baited his trap with. Burlap looked up at me, not comprehending that he was trapped in a horse bridle. All he knew was that he was hungry.

"What the heck?" Mike appeared behind me, wearing his fifth grade dork glasses and three layers of Arctic gear.

"It's that guy I've been telling you about," I said. "This clown shows up everywhere, like a dumb dog that can't find his way home."

"Well, that's probably because he doesn't have a home," Mike said.

"Oh. Well, whose fault is that?"

"Uh-oh," Mike said.

**113**

Burlap was now slumped over the device, shreds of radicchio hanging out of his open mouth.

"The tranquilizer," Mike said. "He's out cold."

"We can't leave him out here like this," I said. "He'll freeze to death."

"You can't bring him into my house," said Mike. He untangled Burlap from the harness. "My parents will want to clean him up and turn him into a tax-paying citizen. We can't have that self-improvement stuff going on while we're trying to find the Zephyr."

"He can go to my house," I said.

We hauled Burlap to his feet and dragged him toward the side gate. I realized that in the past couple of days, I had spent more time in the company of this homeless food grubber than I had in the past year with my own father.

"Come on, bud," I whispered, cringing at the dirt and ice that clung to his ragged jacket. "When you wake up, I'll find you some lima beans and Brussels sprouts."

Alice Thorpe has the softest heart in the world. Which might be why it breaks so easily.

"Oh, Nick," was all Mom said when she saw Burlap sacked out on our sofa. I had prepared a long tale, but she didn't want to hear it. "If we can't take care of the needy during the holidays, when can we?" she said.

Mom shook Burlap into semiconsciousness and

pushed coffee on him. At first he sputtered and moaned, but when he got a real gulp of the stuff, he drained the pot in one sitting. When his eyes were as alert as they ever got, my mother shoved him into the bathroom.

"What are you doing?" I yelled through the door.

"Looking for the good inside all this mess," she yelled back. "I have to believe there's a person here, somewhere."

Under all those rags? I just couldn't imagine it. "Do you need help?"

"I do this for a living, remember?" she yelled louder, now over the noise of the shower. As an emergency room nurse, Mom saw all sorts of people in all sorts of circumstances. But it had never registered with me that she actually had to touch them.

She tossed out Burlap's clothes. "Wash whatever you can and we'll trash the rest," she ordered.

Holding it at arm's length, I walked the pile into the kitchen. Mom had passed me Burlap's old coat, two sweatshirts, a flannel shirt, a thermal undershirt and underpants, gray work pants, and three pairs of ratty socks.

I shoved half the stuff into the washer and kicked the rest into the corner. I had already sprinkled the laundry soap when my training kicked in. Check the pockets. I'd rather stick my hand into a toilet than Burlap's pockets. But I did as my mother had taught me. I pulled out sticks, stones, scraps of broccoli,

**115**

and the mint wrapper that Jill and I had left for Burlap. I kept digging, wrinkling my nose the whole time.

My fingertips tingled, then stung. I yanked my hand out, worried some poisonous spider had taken up residence in Burlap's pants. Then I thought of Mom scrubbing the old boy and realized the least I could do for the sorry soul was to clean his clothes.

I reached in again and pulled out something long and glittering. A shiny cord about four feet long. The cord sparkled like a gold chain. It was too soft to be metal, but too sturdy to be fabric. It glowed in my hand as if it were alive. It weighed almost nothing, but somehow it had real substance.

What was Burlap doing with something so incredible? My stomach sank—he probably had stolen it. Maybe I should show it to Quin. But then, that could get Burlap thrown into jail. Even if Burlap had stolen it, he wouldn't have meant to; the guy could barely get food into his own mouth, let alone deliberately rob someone.

I shoved the cord into my pocket, started the washer, then headed back to our tiny living room.

"Here's your friend, Nick," Mom said. "Didn't he clean up nicely?"

*Nice* is a matter of perspective. Without his tatters, Burlap was a scrawny guy, maybe a little taller than Mike Pillsbury, and just as skinny. What I could see of his face under his now-clean but still-wild beard was surprisingly youthful. Burlap didn't have the deep, life-beaten wrinkles that the other clients at St. Mark's all had; his skin was clear and pink after Mom's scrubbing.

*He's just too unaware to let life wear him down,* I thought. *As innocent as a dumb mutt.*

And as hairy as a gorilla. His hands, which seemed too big for his body, were covered in light brown hair. His head had shaggy curls, uncut but nicely conditioned after his shower. As he shifted in his seat, the robe slipped on his shoulder and I realized his chest and back were covered with tawny hair as well.

"What's his name?" Mom asked.

"No clue," I said. "I call him Burlap. He doesn't seem to talk."

"It's not unusual for . . . street people . . . to have various disabilities," Mom said. "He might be mentally ill or handicapped. Or maybe he's suffered some catastrophe, like a stroke that left him unable to speak. Without a family member to watch out for him . . ."

Mom's eyes filled with tears as she wrapped her arms around me.

"We'll always watch out for each other, right?" she whispered.

"Right," I said, and hugged her back.

Burlap stopped chewing and watched, his eyes more confused than ever.

**117**

# 19

"To WHAT DO WE OWE THiS HONOR?"
Quin boomed. "You aren't due back until Monday
afternoon—Christmas Eve."

"We found this guy in our neighbor's backyard.
Hungry, groggy . . ." I stopped, realizing Quin was
staring. But not at Burlap.

"Allie?" Quin whispered. "Allie Wright?"

"Nigel?" Mom squealed, and leaped into Quin's
arms. As they hugged and kissed, I realized two
things. First, I knew why Quin went by only his last
name—Nigel was an invitation to a whumping.
And second, that Mom's life hadn't started with me
and Dad.

The food line opened. Burlap was off in a shot,
even though we had fed him pancakes and cereal

before driving him to the shelter.

Mom and Quin finally disengaged, still laughing and wiping tears. "Nick," Mom said, surprised, as if she had forgotten I existed. "This is Nigel Quin. We were in nursing school together."

"We've met," I said. "I work here, remember?"

She looked at Quin, her eyes dancing. "Remember the all-nighters, learning our phalanges and tarses?"

"And all that coffee, trying to pry our eyes open? We were walking on the ceiling by daybreak." Quin laughed.

"We did our first needle sticks on each other, remember?" Mom said.

Quin rubbed his backside. "I still have the scars."

"I think I'll go help with breakfast," I stammered.

Troy presided over the eggs and bacon like a talk show host. Didn't the dude ever go home? He hugged each male client like a long-lost brother, straightening their coats and patting their backs and chests. Only Burlap shuffled through the food line without a smile; his face was in his plate almost before he sat down.

"Hey, Nick, how's it going?" Troy smiled.

"What're you, running for president?" I snapped as I threw on an apron and grabbed a spoon. Here I was, trying to do a good deed by helping, and Mr. Perfection beat me to it. "What's with all the butt kissing?"

"I'm just trying to be nice."

"Yeah, well, I guess nice comes easier to some people than others," I grumbled. Strange, none of Jill's boyfriends had ever inspired in me the loathing that Mr. Perfection did.

"Hey, you're working at it. That's all that matters, isn't it?" Troy put his arm around me, patting me down like he had the clients. I pulled away quickly. Troy reeked. What had he been smoking this time?

Better yet, who had he been smoking it with?


A Bom can outstink a Dumpster any day.

"I know you're there," I yelled as I lugged bags of breakfast trash to the Dumpster.

"I'm not *there*. I am *here*." I whipped around to see the Bom sliming down the stone wall of St. Mark's like a giant slug.

"Where are your fire slingers?" I said.

"Doing their job. Hunting for the Zephyr."

"So why don't you stop stinking up this neighborhood and go join them?" I asked.

"I'm about to make you an offer you can't refuse," the Bom huffed. "Listen carefully, Freakface, because this deal is good for the next five minutes, and after that . . ." The Bom snapped his tentacle; a

**120**

spark flipped off its tip. "After that, I cannot be responsible for what my client might do."

"What's this offer?" I asked.

"What do you want most in this world?" the Bom said.

"What're you, Santa Claus?" I sneered.

"Answer the question. What do you want?"

"World peace, an end to hunger, and . . ." I stopped. The Bom could easily give me anything I could imagine. A new house, nicer clothes, Mom not having to work, a car that wasn't held together with duct tape, a college education.

But what I really wanted, no one in the whole universe could give me except Mom and Dad. And that would never happen unless someone could turn back the hands of time.

"I am prepared to see that you get whatever you want," huffed the Bom. "If you will only tell me."

"Hey, Bom?"

"Yes?" The Bom's tentacles straightened as he came to attention.

"What do you call a thousand Boms falling into a black hole?" I asked.

"What?" the Bom said.

"A good start!" I snorted. "Now go stink up someone else's planet."

The Bom burped from all his orifices. "You will be very sorry, Freakface."

"Why don't you and those LizardPukes of yours

**121**

go take a flying leap into hyperspace?" I heaved the bags into the Dumpster and let the top fall with a huge *clang*.

"LizardPukes?" the Bom asked. "Are they related to Boogies? Or Snots?"

"I'm referring to those flying ashtrays of yours. Those lame dragon things . . . you know, your precious Draconians."

The Bom belched with laughter. "Those aren't Draconians, you foolish human. Those are Conflagrons. Ideal for operations on nonsanctioned planets. We don't need to bring weapons that could be detected by native military because the Conflagrons *are* weapons. Delightful creatures, really."

"But Draco . . . Mike Pillsbury says it's the dragon constellation," I stuttered. "I just assumed . . . with the scales and the flames . . ."

"Ah, and that is a universal problem. *People* just assume too much. Just as you may assume that you can string my client along forever. However, Freakface, this is your last chance. Will you turn over the Zephyr?"

"I already gave you my answer," I said, trying to keep my legs from wobbling. "Flying leap, remember?"

"In that case . . . I think you have an expression here on Earth," the Bom huffed.

"Tons of them. Get lost. Drop dead. Make like an egg and beat it," I snarled.

"Ah yes," the Bom said, his face twisting into that pretzel smile. "I believe the expression I was looking for is . . ." He turned a knob on his translator box, and the words echoed off the church's stone walls, each one like a swift kick to my head.

"See you in Hell."

I went into the men's lavatory and barfed my brains out.

Who did I think I was, shielding a dangerous beast from outer space? Bayurd was still in Jill's bedroom. At any moment, an army of Conflagrons could charge in and take the creature by force. Mike's device was no protection against a Bom with a Federation removal order and his army of LizardPukes.

I needed Mike. There were too many questions for my lame brain. If the Bom's fire-breathing enforcers were Conflagrons, then who or what were the Draconians? Were they lurking underfoot or overhead without my even knowing it?

And what proof did I have that the Zephyr was intelligent? Sure, Jill had tamed the creature with a touch. But she didn't get to be Homecoming Princess and Sophomore Class President just on good looks and intelligence. Jill could connect with anyone or anything.

Then there was Mike's Chronicle, which told of Zephyrs as magnificent people when coupled with

**123**

their Garths. But the Sirian had declared that story to be false.

I remembered Mom's words when she cleaned up Burlap in the middle of the night. She was "looking for the good inside all this mess." I had believed there was good inside all this mess of Zephyrs and time warps. So I deceived Mike about the Zephyr and then allowed Jill to join me in the deception. And where had it gotten us?

Mom had showered Burlap, but she hadn't succeeded in washing away his hunger and dimwittedness. She had cleaned up one mess, only to reveal another one underneath.

Was I about to do that?

# 20

**JiLL'S BEDROOM WAS LiTTERED WiTH** empty salad boxes.

Bayurd was stretched out on the floor of her walk-in closet, sound asleep.

Jill stroked his side. Following her fingertips in streams of color, reds and golds danced under his hide. "He's totally exhausted. He's been running for a long time," she said.

"And for a long way," I added. "How come no one has asked how he got to Earth?"

"That's a darn good question. These guys are telling us he's a dumb beast, but they're not offering any explanation about how this critter flew through outer space and ended up here."

"Does he really talk to you, Jill?"

"It's not exactly talking. Things about him just

pop up in my head. Like his name. And that he's very tired and scared. But most of all . . . *stubborn* is not the right word . . . I guess I would say he is determined."

"Determined about what?"

"I don't know," Jill said. "Listening to him, it's like watching the clouds take shape. Sometimes the sun cuts through and his thoughts are honey-colored. But sometimes they form heavy and gray, like storm clouds. And when he's frightened, it's like wisps of vapor, ripped apart by the wind."

"So what do we do?" I asked. "I thought we could turn over the Zephyr to the Sirians and they would protect him. But now . . ."

"Maybe you should call for help again."

"Are you kidding? Look who showed up the first time—a poor imitation of a Chihuahua and a terrific imitation of a garbage heap, complete with his army of trash fires. My record ain't so great, Jill."

"You're not going to give up, are you?"

"Who, me? Run away from a mess when I could make it even worse? Not a chance," I said. "But I'm sorry I dragged you into it."

"Are you kidding?" Jill forced a grin. "Do you know how boring it is, being a Homecoming Princess? This is really living."

Really living. But for how long, I wondered. For how long?

☆　☆　☆

**126**

eSWAP was out. Look at the mess we were in already. But how else could I call for help? Who could I trust? Mike was working for the other side. Schreiber was a football star but a stinky basketball player, so no one was hounding him for interviews just now. Katelyn would side with Mike. Jay Loose was five years old—and besides, he and his family were in Hawaii for the whole month.

I couldn't go to anyone who had not had contact with aliens, especially the police, government, or army. That could result in neutralization for the whole planet.

So I was left with Stacia Caraviello. When I phoned, the maid told me she was out for the afternoon, giving a charity performance at the Community Center. "But you can catch it on the radio," the maid said. "It's going to be broadcast."

Broadcast . . .

I talked Mom into driving me to the center, then I wheeled my way backstage. The Weird Band Girl had been transformed into an elegant young woman in a dark green velvet gown. Stacia's hair was pulled back with a diamond clip and her face was carefully made up in warm, peach tones. Maybe Scott Schreiber wasn't so stupid after all, if he liked a class act like Stacia.

"You needed to see me?" she asked.

"Can you keep a secret?"

"I think I've proven myself," Stacia said with a

smile. "What do you need?"

"Help." I explained about the difference of opinion about the Zephyr. I told her Jill and I had him safe but I wouldn't tell her where we had hidden him. "For your own safety," I said. "Not only are the Boms, Conflagrons, and the mysterious Draconians after him, but even Mike Pillsbury and that weasel Sirian want to find him."

"Even if I wanted to help you," Stacia said, blinking hard, "how can I? I'm not an electronics genius like Mike. Or a hero like Scott."

"But you know how to communicate in ways that none of us do. Mike told me how you subdued a whole fleet of Shards by playing your violin. Please, Stacia. I know you don't know me very well . . . but you know . . ."

"I know that the universe is filled with surprises," she said softly. "I'll give it my best, okay?"

Stacia's best was out of this world.

Raised on rock TV and Mom's show tunes, I had never heard anything like the music Stacia performed that afternoon. Reading the program was like reading a foreign language. But when she began to play her violin, a world opened up inside me that I had never known existed.

For over an hour I almost forgot about time warps and LizardPukes and Zephyrs and divorces. Then Stacia laid down her violin. "I'd like to play a little tune for a special friend," she said.

She picked up a strange-looking instrument—a battered violin held together by what looked like medical tape. It was strung with glittering metallic wire. I realized it was the fiddle that Mike had told me about, the one whose music saved the Lyra and maybe even Earth from the Shards. The metal strings were from the Lyra's nest, but the ability to communicate with the stars was all in Stacia's hands.

As Stacia drew her bow, the strings made a zinging sound. I stifled a laugh; the people in the audience giggled, suddenly quite amused.

As Stacia played on, a story formed in my head.

*A horse with a horn flies on the wind, the stars under his feet. His head is proud and his colors are true.*

*A funny boy and a beautiful girl run after the horse. The girl catches him, braiding her fingers in his mane. The boy holds the girl's hand and the horse pulls the two of them along, sparks kicking up under their feet as they try to keep to the ground.*

*Thick wings beat with fury, fanning the sparks. The world catches fire. The flames disgorge hideous beasts who speak more fire. The boy and the girl wither with heat and fear. The horned horse bucks, wanting to flee. But he won't leave the boy and the girl.*

*Even if he could, there is no place left to run.*

*Ahead, there is a black unknown so bottomless even the stars lose their light.*

*The girl tightens her grip on the horned horse and the boy tightens his grip on the girl. The boy loves the horse and the boy loves the girl.*

*The flames lick at them. The beasts fly overhead, mocking with sparks and flares.*

*The boy raises his hands to the sky, asking for cool water to dowse the flames.*

*Longing sweeps over them like a wave—a longing to chase the horizon, where the sky is cool and welcoming.*

*The boy raises his hands higher, waiting.*

*Time stands still.*

There was a stunned silence when Stacia put down her bow.

"Sorry," Stacia said, her voice soft. "It's a little different . . ."

"Sorry?" someone cried out. "It's brilliant! Bravo!" The audience erupted with applause. Stacia bowed, her eyes locked on mine.

*Thank you,* I mouthed.

"Encore!" someone shouted, and it became a chorus.

Stacia picked up her concert violin and fiddled a rousing "Joy to the World."

As I pushed out of the auditorium, I hoped and prayed it would be joy and not terrible trouble.

# 21

THERE WAS A POLICE CAR IN FRONT OF the Pillsbury house. I ran inside, fearing the worst.

Pam Pillsbury was freaking out in the front hall. Jill sat on the stairs, rolling her eyes and twiddling her thumbs. Mike sat behind her, his eyes cool and focused on something far away. I knew he was thinking.

"What's wrong?" I asked.

"Someone stole our Christmas tree!" Pam moaned. "Is nothing sacred?"

A patrolman stood silent, confused. A man in a tweed jacket, who I assumed was a detective, bit back a grin.

"Grand larceny!" Dana Pillsbury stated.

"I think this . . . um, incident . . . falls more into the category of petty theft," the detective said. He kept a poker face, but his belly shook with giggles.

"The Pillsbury Christmas tree is the centerpiece of our holiday decor!" Pam sniffed. "We worked with a professional decorator, surely you've heard of her—Madame Durette? We spent a thousand dollars on the presentation, and look . . ." With a sob, she dramatically flung open the door to the living room.

The ornate brass tree stand stood empty. Strangely, the tree's costly ornaments and its strings of two thousand lights were piled carefully in heaps on the floor.

"Not only did the thief take our tree," Dana snarled, "but he also took all our houseplants!"

"Not necessarily *he*, dear," Pam interrupted. "Women can be just as good at thievery as men can. Which may explain why *she* also took the herbs I was cultivating on the kitchen windowsill!"

"Not necessarily *she*, dear," Dana corrected. "Men can be just as good at herbal cuisine as women."

The detective shook from head to foot, trying to keep his laughter inside.

"The point is, Detective," Pam continued, "the thief has taken every living green thing from our home!"

Every living green thing.

Mike and I shot each other a glance, then booked it out of the living room. He headed for the backyard, while I went back into the front hall. Jill sat on the stairs, flirting with the patrolman.

"We have to talk," I said. Jill flashed a Homecoming Princess smile at the cop. He unconsciously flexed; his muscles bulged under his uniform jacket.

Jill followed me to the back porch. We watched Mike crunching through the snow to his Zephyr catcher.

"What happened?" I whispered.

"I fell asleep," Jill said with a sigh. "Bayurd got hungry. So . . ."

"He ate the Christmas tree?" I squealed.

Jill smacked my arm. "Shhhh. Keep your voice down. Yes, he ate every green thing in the house, including Dad's Chia pets and that fungus Mike was growing for science."

"Oh, great," I said. "The police are going to search the house and find him."

"No. They're not." Jill smiled. "He's in your garage."

"Oh, double great. He'll go nuts and buck everything to pieces."

"Stop your whining," Jill said. "He swore he'd be good."

"I thought he didn't use words," I said.

"Well, it was more letting me see a picture of waving grasses and feeling tired and full and just wanting to sleep," Jill explained. Then she frowned. "Watch out! Here comes Albert."

Mike stepped up on the porch. "Darn," he said. "I thought we had him."

"He wasn't in your Zephyr catcher?" I asked.

"No. He trashed the house but stayed clear of the trap." Mike frowned.

"Pretty smart for a dumb beast," I sneered.

Titan stuck his sniveling nose out of Mike's jacket. The rat had been hiding in Mike's pocket, true hero that he was. "He got lucky," the Sirian said. "Despite your delusions, Freakface, he is a dumb beast."

Mike's face shone with determination. "And I will catch him."

"Suppose you do. Will you do what is right? Or will you do what you're told?" I stared icicles at Mike.

He stared daggers back. "Have you ever considered that they might be the same thing? Or do you refuse to acknowledge any authority?"

"I bend my back to no one," I whispered, keeping my gaze steady.

Mike blinked.

Mom hummed all evening. "It was wonderful, seeing Nigel Quin again. And, of course, Ivy. Did you know Nigel's mother was once a television star?"

"I kind of guessed that," I said. "She's pretty flashy for a short-order cook."

"Soaps," Mom said. "She was big in her time."

"If the Quins have a lot of money, why do they work at the shelter?"

"Nigel has always had a big heart," Mom said. "He gets it from Ivy. When Nigel and his sisters came along, she left her glamorous career to stay home with the kids. I thought she was crazy—until you were born. Then I understood."

"Um," I said, my mouth full of french fries. I was saving my salad for Bayurd, left on his own in the garage. I didn't want him chewing my green bike or Mr. Loose's putting green.

"Nick." Mom's voice shifted into that *mother* tone. "I talked to your father today. Things are still lousy with his job. Money is very tight for him. But there is some good news here. It seems the hospital is understaffed and I can pick up as much overtime as my feet can stand. If I work sixty hours this week and next, I can make enough money to buy you that plane ticket to Arizona."

Arizona. Blue sky and sunshine.

"No," I said. "Don't."

"But you were looking forward to seeing your father . . ."

"I don't want to have to give up seeing you, too. It's the holiday season. You shouldn't have to work all the time."

Mom patted my shoulder. "You're busy with school, your friends. And now you're working at the shelter. You won't miss me."

"Yes. I will."

"Nick, I'd really like to do this for you," she said. "I know you had your heart set on a change of scenery."

I looked around at our tiny kitchen with its cheap wallpaper and curtains made out of bed-sheets. "Forget the overtime. And forget the scenery. Things are okay just the way they are."

"What brought this about?"

I stirred my ketchup with a soggy fry. "Lots of things." I couldn't tell her about the slippery Bom or the nasty Conflagrons or the traitorous Sirians. Nor could I tell her about the Zephyr, right under her feet, in the garage.

"I guess . . . Burlap," I mumbled. "Someone with nothing . . . makes you appreciate what you've got."

"Oh, yes. Your friend. You know what, Nick?"

"What?"

"We may not look it," Mom said, "but you and I are very rich."

"You know what, Mom?"

"What?"

"I agree." I grinned.

# 22

BAYURD FEASTED ON MY SPINACH salad like it was cookie-dough ice cream.

The garage was musty and dark. It was filled with all the furniture that fit in our four-bedroom house but not in our little apartment. The windows were partially blocked with wood, paint cans, and garden tools. No one ever came in here; it was the kind of place where you stuffed things and then forgot about them.

A perfect place to hide a Zephyr—as long as he remained quiet.

"I know it's not the nice meadow you're used to," I said. "Hey, maybe you'd never even seen snow before you came to Earth. I'll have to ask Mike . . ." Flush that idea; I couldn't ask Mike anything. Not while he was working for the other side.

Bayurd walked to the door and pressed his nose against it.

"No," I said. "You can't go out there. The Bom and his Conflagrons are gunning for you. Mike and that stupid Titan are on your tail, too."

The Zephyr butted his head against the wood, sending a *crack* through the garage like a lightning snap.

"Don't do that!" I hissed. "My mom will hear you! And she can't know about you. Please, you have got to be quiet or you could get my whole planet neutralized."

The creature reared his head back, ready to strike again. I grabbed his mane. He froze, his eyes glowing like molten steel. "Please. You promised Jill." His eyes flickered, cooling slightly. "Jill and I . . . we're your friends. We're trying to help you. Why won't you let us?" I stroked his neck, watching the colors flow. "Why won't you talk to me like you do to Jill? Maybe it would help."

The Zephyr leaned his neck into my hand. His muscles quivered with power. The hair of his mane flowed through my fingers, glowing and alive.

Something tumbled in my brain, something about the way the Zephyr's mane tingled in my hand—but I couldn't catch the thought. There were other thoughts, crowding mine out. . . .

*I had never been alone before. My feet were lighter than air. I flew over the grass and rocks and rivers, like memories easily left behind.*

*I flew faster than the light, moving into the shadows of night like a comet. Racing now faster than the stars, faster than the universe as it beat outward, like a mighty heart pounding with life.*

*I flew faster than what is and became what will be. Darkness.*

*My heart almost stopped. I was seized with a fear that I had seen the Endless Ways and they were without meaning. Then a light flickered, a thought wandering in the vastness, asking the same questions. Why am I here? What is expected of me? Does anyone care?*

*And then I realized the darkness wasn't an end but a beginning, that the unknown would be filled with light, a light that I could bring.*

*If only someone would show me the way . . .*

"I don't know," I whispered, leaning my head against Bayurd's face. "I don't know the way any better than you do. But at least we're not alone, are we?"

My face was wet. I dabbed my eyes—was I crying? No, my eyes were dry. My fingers sparkled with dampness. I looked into the Zephyr's eyes.

They were leaking sadness and moonlight.

*WAH-WAH-WAH* split my head like a missile, blasting me out of a deep sleep. I couldn't move, couldn't see, couldn't breathe. Thick smoke

**139**

smothered me like a lead blanket.

*How boring,* I thought as I drowned in a sea of gray. *I wanted to go out in a blaze of glory, but instead I'm just going to fade away.*

"Nick!" My mother's voice shrilled over the smoke alarm. "Get up!"

*Just let me drift,* I wanted to say, but I couldn't find the air to form words. *I'm so tired of ducking and running.*

Just as the gray bled into black, a hand jerked me out of bed. A world gone mad assaulted me. Gray smoke. Orange flames. Choking fumes. Snapping fire. Hot, hot, unbearably hot.

I felt myself pulled along. I resisted, my mind fighting to comprehend what I was about to leave behind. Baseball cards, comic books, pictures of Mom and Dad, my favorite cap.

"Nick, you've got to help me," Mom cried, her voice harsh. "Fight!" I could feel her hands now, rough and strong, pushing me. Then I was hit with an icy slap. I instinctively pulled back to the heat but the fire behind me flared from the fresh fuel brought in by the night air. Too cold one way, too hot the other.

Mom pushed me out the door, then half carried me down the stairs.

Sirens wailed, far away, then closer. Lights flashed everywhere—flames shooting, sparks exploding, flashlights bobbing. Dana and Pam and

Mike rushed at us. Mom pushed me at Dana, then collapsed against Pam. Dana wrapped me in a blanket, then passed me to Jill so he could help Mom.

Mike ran down the driveway, waving his arms, trying to clear away the neighbors as the fire trucks grew closer.

Jill's hair glowed red with fire. "Bayurd," she whispered. "Is he still in there?"

"Yes!" I moaned. "He can't die, not this way." I wanted to go to him but my legs wouldn't work.

Jill dashed toward the fire. Our apartment roared with flames jumping from windows, slashing through the roof. But the downstairs garage just smoldered, clouding with heavy smoke. Then, from somewhere inside myself, I heard the Zephyr's cry. *Let me run so I can go out in a blaze of glory.*

Seconds later I was next to Jill, tugging on the door that I had locked to protect the Zephyr. The key was upstairs, now melted beyond recognition, and the Zephyr was still inside, about to be consumed if we didn't get him out.

I slammed a rock through the window. Behind me, red lights flashed. The fire trucks had found us and would be down the driveway in seconds. Jill and I both reached through the broken glass, trying to find the bolt. Under the mighty voice of the fire, something clicked—Jill had opened the latch. The door popped open.

The Zephyr charged out, his eyes a whirlwind of

silver and fear. "No!" I yelled, but in a flash of light we disappeared, my mother's cries echoing behind us.

"Where's my son?"

# 23

THIRTY MINUTES LASTED AN EXCRU-
ciating eternity.

Jill's watch read 11:35 P.M.; the clock in my mother's car read 12:05 A.M. With the fire closing in on us, Bayurd had only knocked us into the near future. We didn't have much time to wait until we returned to *now*.

But it was the worst time of my life.

Jill's parents and my mom knew we were missing. They were frozen in pure panic, straining against the firefighters who held them back. Though we were only a breath away, there was nothing we could do to soothe them.

"I can't stand looking at them another second," Jill sobbed. "Let's find someplace to hide Bayurd."

I couldn't even answer her. My throat and lungs felt like they had been scraped with sandpaper. *Where?* I mouthed.

"The shed behind St. Mark's," Jill said. "Where they store the nativity set. They set the manger up this weekend, so the shed is empty."

*The Bom hangs out there,* I wanted to cry. But, of course! The Bom wouldn't expect us to hide the Zephyr right under his nose.

I nodded. Jill grasped Bayurd's mane and jerked his face to hers. "This would be a whole lot easier if you would let us ride you," she said.

He bucked, his eyes flashing.

Jill stamped her foot. "You're worse than a mule. Look at all of this! Why are you being so difficult?"

The Zephyr looked at the devastation—my home in flames, Mom and Dana and Pam in frozen panic. His eyes flickered and his head dropped, as if in guilt. But his back stayed straight.

"Fine," Jill said. "Have it your way!" She jogged down the driveway, turning her face away so she didn't have to look at the terrified stares on her parents' faces.

The Zephyr trotted after her. I tried to follow, but—*SMACK*—I was on my face. Jill ran back and picked me up. "You okay?"

I nodded yes. But I still couldn't get moving.

"You'll have to stay here," she said. "You're wiped out."

**144**

"What do I tell them"—I forced the words through my raw throat—"about where you are?"

"You'll think of some stupid story." Jill grinned. "You always do."

She disappeared down the street, leading the Zephyr through a scene frozen in time. Our horrified families, the intense firemen, and our concerned neighbors all watched the fire, stunned and clearly fearing the worst. The streams of water from the hose were like solid ropes, the truck lights beacons of red. Even the flames were frozen, fingers of brilliant yellow and blue and white, tearing my home apart. Red embers shot upward, the only color in the billows of smoke and water vapor that covered the sky.

Inside the murky cloud, something dark and mighty moved. The Conflagrons hovered over our garage like fire-spitting vultures. They had been swept into the time warp with us.

Frantic, I looked for Jill, but she and the Zephyr seemed to have already turned the corner. My shouts came out as raspy squeaks.

I limped down the road after them, then fell. My face smashed into the hard pavement, sharp with chunks of ice and road salt. I tried to get back up, but I felt as if my legs were on another planet.

*Watch out*, I cried inside my head. *Jill, please watch out.*

☆   ☆   ☆

**145**

"Watch out!" someone shouted through the hum of time and motion that meant I was back in *now*.

A police car squealed to a stop, its tires only a few feet from my head. I lay facedown on the road, my mind still spinning with winged dragons and running horses and Jill.

"Here he is!" someone shouted. Hands gently rolled me onto my side. Lights flashed in my eyes. I blinked and coughed, then couldn't stop choking. Someone put a plastic mask over my mouth. Cold, pure air flooded in, easing the pain in my lungs.

Then my mother was on me, crying and laughing.

"Our stuff "—I croaked—"gone."

She pulled me tight. "I've got you. Nothing else matters."

Over her shoulder, I saw the panicked faces of Pam and Dana Pillsbury. Mike, fighting back tears, was pushing through the crowd, searching for Jill.

"Jill . . ." I rasped, pulling the oxygen mask aside.

"We can't find her," Pam whispered, then sagged against Dana. They held each other up.

"She's okay," I said, each word ripping my raw throat. "McCoy's dog . . . its tail caught fire and it ran down the road. She ran after it, to take care of it. I tried to help, but—"

"Hush," my mother whispered. Pam and Dana looked somewhat relieved, though I knew they

**146**

wouldn't relax until Jill had come back from her mission of mercy.

If the LizardPukes hadn't caught up with her.

Mike stared at me as if he was trying to see inside my head. He had known me forever; sometimes he could do that. So I pushed images of Jill being chased by those winged beasts out of my head. I tried to see her chasing the McCoys' mutt, but somehow all I could see was Jill running.

Mike grimaced, then finally turned away.

Mom and I were loaded into ambulances so the paramedics could check us over. Pam headed down the street to look for Jill. Dana hustled about, trying to supervise the firemen. After a few minutes, Jill jumped into the ambulance with me.

"What took you so long?" I said.

"The door to the shed was closed. So I had to wait at St. Mark's until we were back in *now* to open it and put Bayurd inside. I got back here as soon as I could. What did you tell my parents?"

I whispered our cover story to Jill. She smiled, then backed out of the ambulance.

Mike blocked her way. "Where's the Zephyr?"

"Sorry, you moron," Jill snapped. "But I don't have time to play your silly fantasy games right now. If you hadn't noticed, the Thorpes' apartment just burned down."

"I noticed, all right," Mike said. "Are you two

**147**

going to wait until the Draconians burn down the whole town before you turn over the Zephyr?"

Anger roared up in me like the flames that had taken my home. "Not Draconians!" I rasped. "You don't know everything, Mike! Draconians don't breathe fire. It's those Conflagrons who did this!" Then I collapsed back on the stretcher. No, Mike didn't know everything. But now he knew one more thing. He knew about the Conflagrons. Which meant he knew another thing.

He knew that I knew more than I was telling.

# 24

MOM AND I WERE OFFICIALLY HOMELESS.

Fearing a gas leak, the fire chief had evacuated the neighborhood. The Pillsburys and other families were spending what was left of the night with relatives or in a hotel. Mom had balked—we just couldn't afford a hotel, especially now. Dana wanted to pay for us, but pride wouldn't let us accept his generosity.

So Mom and I headed for St. Mark's. We arrived with nothing but the clothes on our backs. Fortunately, I had fallen asleep in my jeans and sweatshirt; otherwise, the whole world would know that I still wore cartoon character pajamas.

Mom and Quin huddled over coffee in the shelter's kitchen, Quin cracking stupid jokes and Mom forcing a grin. I sat on the counter, slowly munching a bowl of cereal. I dreaded going into the men's bunkroom but I was too old to be spending the night with the women and young children.

"Hey, Nick!" Quin motioned me over. "Why don't you put your mom's stuff in a locker for the night? Then you should think about hitting the sack." We had stopped by the emergency room to get checked out, and Mom had changed into some surgical scrubs. Showing up at the shelter in her nightgown just didn't seem cool, though I knew clients showed up in far worse.

Quin handed me a plastic bag with Mom's clothes and took me to his office to get the key to the storage room.

"You okay, Nick? It's been a rough night for you," Quin said.

"Why wouldn't I be okay?" I asked. "I'm always okay." I turned away from Quin so he couldn't see how *not* okay I was.

Quin's hand on my shoulder was strong but somehow comforting. "You've worked here long enough now to know that it's not what we *have* that's important. It's what we *are*."

"So what am I? The best friend of a kid who won't believe a word I say," I whispered. "The son of two parents who can't stay together for five minutes without getting in a fight."

Quin gently pulled on my shoulder so I'd have to turn and look at him. "You try hard, Nick. But you can't hide what you really are."

"The class clown. The school screwup, " I whispered. I couldn't look at Quin.

"Compassionate. Intelligent. Strong. Funny as all get out. So stop selling yourself short."

I nodded, took the key, and headed for the locker room.

Even after I passed through the kitchen and dining room, I could somehow still feel Quin's hand on my shoulder.

The shelter was in semidarkness. The men's bunkroom echoed with snoring, grunting, and mumbling. Quin had said the homeless tended to be uneasy sleepers, fearing that someone would rob or hurt them while they slept.

I decided I would stay up for the rest of the night. I stifled a yawn as I slipped the key in the lock. Then I stopped.

Someone was inside.

*Now would be a good time to run*, I warned myself. So I opened the door.

Troy was digging through the clients' lockers like a dog looking for a bone.

"Lose something?" I snapped. "Your smokes, maybe?"

Troy whirled around. "Just doing some cleaning."

"In the middle of the night?"

"Best time to get things done." He grinned.

"Don't you agree?"

"Does Quin know you're here?" I asked.

"He's a busy man, he can't know everything."

Troy pushed past me, heading for the door. I grabbed his arm. His biceps flexed defensively under his shirt. He had a teenager's face but a man's muscles.

*Now would be a good time to shut up and just let him go.* But I was in no mood to bend my back to anyone. "What are you looking for?" I said.

"Just doing my job." Troy smiled, trying to pull away.

I gripped tighter. "This isn't a job. You're a stupid volunteer, just like me."

Troy's face went cold. "I am nothing like you, you puny Freakface." He yanked out of my grasp as if I were no stronger than a puff of smoke.

I slept in a chair in the shower room. Mom shook me awake at 7 A.M. "The fire chief called," she said. "The gas lines have been checked and everyone can go home."

"What home?" I mumbled, trying to work the sleep out of my eyes and the knots out of my back.

"We're going to stay in our old house while the Looses are in Hawaii," Mom said. "Let's go."

I staggered into the dining room to find a Christmas tree under construction. Quin was balanced on a ladder, stringing lights. Ivy was serving hot chocolate with red and green bagels.

"What's all this?" I asked.

"We're getting ready for our annual Christmas party." Quin beamed. "The kids will be arriving this afternoon to see Santa and get their presents." He jumped off the ladder. "For most of them, it's the only Christmas they'll have."

I finally allowed myself to think about the Christmas we wouldn't have: our tree, decorated with ornaments that Mom and I had made; the navy wool blazer I had saved all fall for so Mom could have a nice suit jacket; the cookies Mom had baked last week; the holiday cards that had been arriving since Thanksgiving.

Our Christmas had gone up in flames, along with the rest of our life.

"Why don't you come for the party, Allie?" Quin boomed. "We serve a nice buffet and sing lots of carols. Maybe Nick can help hand out the presents. Might even find something under that tree for himself."

*No,* I wanted to yell. *I don't need charity from a homeless shelter.*

"We'd love to," Mom said, smiling.

I just walked out, without a good-bye. Or a thank-you.

I threw myself down on Jay Loose's bed. There was no trace of me left in my old bedroom. Jay's mother had decorated in teddy bears, which Jay had hidden under posters of quasars and spaceships and worm-faced aliens.

The phone rang. My bones, haunted by last night's *WAH-WAH-WAH*, almost jumped through my skin. The phone kept ringing and ringing; I figured Mom must have gone outside for a minute.

I picked up the receiver. "What!"

"Nick?"

The voice on the other end was muddy, too far away. "Who is this?" I asked.

"It's Dad."

I hadn't even recognized his voice.

"Nick, I was so worried. Your mom called this morning. Are you all right?"

"We're fine, Dad. Just . . . a little freaked, that's all."

"I'm coming out there. I'll get a flight this afternoon."

My heart leaped. But then I came back down to Earth. "You can't, Dad. Mom told me things were really bad with your job. You don't have the money, especially with the new baby coming."

"You're still my kid, too," Dad said. "I'll find the money, borrow it, sell one of the cars, whatever. Quit the stupid job if I can't get the time off. But I need to make sure you're all right."

And suddenly, I *was* all right. "Dad, stay there," I said. "Maybe we can figure out how to get me there

**154**

for vacation. But don't make things any worse for yourself or"—I usually choked on the words, but now they came freely—"Beverly and Sara and Tara."

We talked for another twenty minutes. Big things, like the fire. Little things, like how Ashby had won the Super Bowl last month but our basketball team stunk. Funny things, like how my half sisters would rather play with their potty than use it. When I hung up, I felt better than I had in a long time.

I lay back down on Jay's bed, now calm and sleepy. I rolled onto my side, trying to get comfortable. Something nagged at my hip. Burlap's golden cord, still in my pocket. I fingered it, thinking how some things can be bent and stretched—like my Dad and me—but never broken.

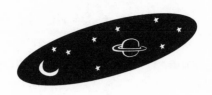

## 25

i WALKED ON A RiBBoN oF LiGHT. i had been walking forever, yet I wasn't tired, wasn't lost, wasn't angry. Somehow it had all been left behind and what remained was a shining road to Always.

Music soared around me. So deep at times, it surged through my body like a powerful wave. Other times it was so high, I felt like I could fly on its moving notes. The music of the stars, I knew, though I had never heard it before.

After I had walked for an age and a half, a companion joined me. He flickered and flowed, with no shape but all substance.

"Where did you come from?" I asked.

"Nowhere. Everywhere." He spoke with no voice but all conviction.

"Where do you live?"

"Never and ForEver."

"Why are you here?" I asked. Though my feet were steady, my head was beginning to spin.

"There is no place to run," he said.

"You came to help me!" I cried.

"If you are the boy who loves the horse and loves the girl."

"Yes, I . . . wait, what do you mean, loves the girl?"

"If you are the boy who loves the horse and loves the girl," he repeated, with no force but all power.

The girl? Where did he get that idea? Of course, Stacia had played it on her funny fiddle during her concert. When the story popped in my head, I thought the part about loving the girl was a slip of the bow or a joke on Stacia's part. Anyone who knew me knew that Jill had been tormenting me as long as she had been tormenting her brother.

How could that be love? We were always in each other's faces. I endured every boyfriend Jill paraded by us; Jill endured every insult I hurled. She was everything I was not—smart, popular, attractive, sure of herself.

But last night, she had come back to pick me up.

I looked down at the shining path and saw Jill's bright hair and her lively eyes and her helping hands. She outshone the stars.

"Yes, I am the boy who loves the horse and loves the girl. So what do I do to protect them? Can you

**157**

come back with me and make that stupid Sirian see reason? Or maybe you have some weapon I can borrow?"

"Look at this," he said, with a wave of no hand but all direction.

"Is it a world?" I asked, realizing for the first time that there was no down and all up.

"We are Out of Time," he said with no logic but all reason. "There is no matter as you know it. But all matters."

"I'm sorry." I staggered, almost falling off the path. "I don't understand."

"Look at this," he said again. Ribbons of light, in all colors and tones and notes, stretched in every direction but always onward.

"What are they?" I asked.

"The Endless Paths."

"Where do they go?"

"Truth, strife, hope, despair, love, peace, anger, joy," he said.

Below me was a wide space where a path should be. The space was completely empty. I never knew nothing could be so terrifying. "What is that one?" I asked.

"That is the absence of good. Evil," he said. "Though it goes nowhere, it is well traveled."

The spinning in my head grew worse. I missed time and I missed matter. My path grew purple; I now walked in despair. "How does any of this help me?"

"Know this," he said, with no feeling but all caring. "Sometimes the best step forward is one step backward."

"I don't understand," I said, tired and burdened.

"You don't need to understand," he said, racing away on a path as silver as moonlight. "You just need to believe."

That afternoon I cornered Mike and the Sirian in the treehouse.

"Jill and I have the Zephyr," I said.

"I knew it!" Mike cried. "Turn him over to Titan before we all get killed."

*A world gone mad. Gray smoke. Orange flames. Choking fumes. Snapping fire.*

"No! Not unless Titan gets the Federation to reopen the case and see that the Zephyrs are people, too."

Titan sniffed. "When the Draconians won, we forced an appeal, just to be sure. But a second investigation yielded the same results. The Zephyrs are beasts and they are dangerous."

"You're wrong. You were supposed to help me, Titan," I said calmly. "But you're the one who has put us in danger by refusing to take our side."

"What would you have me do?" Titan growled. "Ignore the Federation custody order? Ignore the evidence that the Draconians provided, showing a massacre? Turn my back on the truth?"

"I would have you look for the real truth." I stared at Titan; his black eyes fixed on mine. I slipped my hand into my jeans pocket, wrapping my fingers around Burlap's golden cord. Neither of us blinked for the longest time.

Then Titan dropped his head. "I'm sorry. I have to do what I think is best."

It was my turn to blink. I didn't want Mike to see the tears.

"Where are you going?" Mike said as I headed for the ladder.

"To do what I have to," I said, with no clue but all determination.

"Wait!" He grabbed me back. "Why are you being so stubborn about this?"

I pulled my hand out of my pocket, the cord still tangled in my fingers. I had intended to yank Mike's hand off my shoulder but when I touched him, he clasped his hand over mine.

"Life is always a joke to you," he said. "Why are you taking this so seriously?"

The cord felt like an electric wire in my hand. "I know that the Zephyr is intelligent. I know that something bad has happened to him and something worse is about to happen to him—and maybe all of us, if we don't help him."

"How?" Mike whispered. "How do you know?"

The cord was hot in our hands, but we still kept our weird clasp. Thirteen years of friendship tied us together and wouldn't let us go.

"I don't know," I said. "I just believe. And, in case you haven't noticed, Mike . . . because I believe, I haven't ducked and run."

"No, you haven't," Mike said, his eyes clear and intelligent. He was looking right through me, judging me.

This time I didn't come up short.

# 26

**MiKE THREW TiTAN oFF THE PLANET.**
Not a pretty sight, but it sure was funny.

"But . . . but . . ." Titan sputtered. "No one refuses our help. We're a nonprofit, nonsectarian, galactarian—"

"Ad nauseam organization." I yawned. "Been there, puked that."

"Go away!" Mike said. "You're not supposed to be here, anyway. So get lost before I call the army or the navy"—Mike paused, then smiled—"or the Judge."

The Judge had visited Mike with the first round of aliens and had spared him from neutralization on the condition that Mike never call for help again. I had never seen the Judge personally, and based on Mike's description, I didn't want to.

Neither did Titan. "You wouldn't call the Judge!" Titan snarled. "You'd be in terrible trouble!"

"Which I would blame on you," Mike said with a laugh. "Hey, maybe I could call a Bom and sue you for harassment."

"Fine," Titan said. "I'll leave you to the Bom and the Conflagrons and the Draconians."

"What Draconians?" I sneered. "They don't dare show their faces around here."

"They're probably here right now!" Titan said.

"I haven't seen one!" I said.

"You fool! A Draconian could be among you right now, and you wouldn't know it. They look just like humans." Titan's translator box hiccuped. "Except more attractive."

"What?" Something itched in the back of my mind. "What do you mean, more attractive?"

"Among humanoid forms, Draconians are considered to be extraordinarily handsome. In fact, by your standards, a Draconian would be quite perfect."

Titan turned his tail and left the treehouse.

"Quite p-perfect . . ." I stuttered. "Where's Jill?"

"What?" Mike said. "What's the matter now?"

"Tell me where she is!" I bellowed.

"She went to St. Mark's for the Christmas party. With that guy . . . what's his name?"

"Troy," I whispered. "Mr. Perfection."

"Mr. Perfection?" Mike went pale. "Do you think . . ."

"You heard Titan. By human standards, who is more perfect than a Draconian? Now consider this: by Jill standards, who is more perfect than Mr. Perfection himself? Old Troy, who seemed to drop out of nowhere and appear everywhere?"

"Oh, shoot!" Mike flung open the tarp and shouted his brains out. "Titan! Come back!"

The whiff of vapor above the old elm tree told us that Titan had already left the planet, without a good-bye.

Or a forwarding address.

As we raced to St. Mark's, I filled Mike in on the past couple of days. How we had captured, then befriended, the Zephyr. The Bom's threats. The assault and escape at the tennis courts. Even how we had kept tripping over Burlap. I ended with the visit the night before from the creature who was Out of Time.

*There is no matter as you know it. But all matters. . . .*

"Pretty deep stuff. I don't know whether to congratulate you or knock your lights out," Mike said. "Look what it's cost you. Your house. And now my sister could be hanging out with a perfectly handsome and perfectly loathsome Draconian. You should have consulted me on all of this."

"I did ask for your help," I said simply.

Mike skidded to a stop. "You did. And I was a jerk. I'm sorry."

St. Mark's was a Winter Wonderland. Christmas carols filled the air; even Jumpin' Joe was singing his heart out. The tree was hung with sparkling lights, candy canes, and colorful ornaments that the kids had made.

"It makes our thousand-dollar Christmas tree look so fake," Mike said. "I'm glad the Zephyr ate the stupid thing."

Under the tree was a huge pile of presents donated by people and businesses in the community. Santa Claus was scheduled to arrive any moment. I had assumed Quin would be playing the role, but I saw him across the room serving eggnog and holiday cheer. Mom was beside him, smiling bravely.

Jill sat near the tree, reading *The Night Before Christmas* to a circle of kids. A little boy climbed into her lap and Jill kissed the top of his head. The tree lights reflected in her hair like stars.

I loved her so much, it hurt to breathe.

Jill looked up and waved. I waved back. But her eyes were looking past us. I followed her gaze to my left and saw Troy, leaning against the wall. Reeking with perfection and, no doubt, smoke.

Mike and I surrounded Troy, grabbing his arms. His muscles were like steel, but I didn't give a fig. I knew that the Conflagrons and the Bom were acting on behalf of the Draconians. Therefore, this was the creep who had ordered Mom and me burned out of our home.

"You scum-sucking, Bom-kissing son-of-a-Loapher," I growled. "Why don't you go back to where you came from?"

"What? And miss all the fun?" Troy sneered. "You Earthlings sure know how to make merry. Besides, I haven't gotten my Christmas present yet."

"The Sirian has gone back to court to appeal the custody order." Mike lied. "So why don't you back off for a few eons and let the law decide this?"

Troy laughed. "What does the law have to do with any of this?"

"But you w-went to c-court . . ." Mike stuttered.

"That was just to get permission to hang around here on Earth without those bleeding-heart Sirians protesting. By the time I'm done, any law will be meaningless except what I decree."

"You are so full of crap!" I yelped.

Jill startled, glancing up at us. I put my arm around Troy and pretended we were play wrestling. She smiled, happy to see us getting along so well.

As soon as she looked away, Troy twisted, then flipped me into a headlock.

"And you are just so unbelievably stupid," the Draconian said. "Don't you understand? Once I control the Zephyr, I'll control Time. And when I control Time, I will control everything."

**166**

"What?" I yanked out of his grip. "What are you talking about?"

"The horn . . ." Mike gasped. "Zephyrs don't have horns . . . but this one . . ."

Troy's eyes sparkled as he nodded at Mike. "Well, an Earthling with half an ounce of sense."

"With that horn, he's no ordinary Zephyr, is he?" Mike asked.

"The Zephyrs are incredible folks, there's no doubt to that," Troy said. "Faster than any living thing. But once in a million generations, a Zephyr is born with a horn."

"The horn . . . it cuts through the space-time continuum, doesn't it?" Mike said.

"Well done, Pillsbury! You're not half dumb for a resident of this backward planet."

"Mike, what are you talking about?" I said.

"The Zephyr's horn . . . somehow it has the power to magnify the speed of the Zephyr into something that transcends Einsteinian physics," Mike said.

"In English, you geek!"

"The horn lets him rip through ordinary space and step into the next dimension. Into Time. Which is why he keeps bumping you into the future. Obviously, he doesn't know how to control his power, so he just charges forward—not just in space, but also in Time."

"That's because he needs a rider!" I said.

"He *has* a rider!" Troy snapped. "When I get my

hands on that creature, I will ride him places you can't even conceive of. And I will do things you can't even imagine."

"He'll never bend his back to you!" I hissed.

"True, he has been resisting the notion. The whole race is as stubborn as mules. Unfortunate trait. We would have left the rest of them alone, if they had only turned over the beast with the horn. But they insisted on protecting him. Forcing us into that massacre on Grayle," Troy fumed.

"The one where the Draconians were allegedly trampled?" Mike asked.

"Oh, my people were trampled all right. Along with hundreds of Conflagron mercenaries we hired to support our efforts. Even with the Conflagron firepower and Draconian superior intelligence, we experienced some losses. But it was worth it. We were able to . . . shall we say . . . *liberate* the Zephyrs from their Garth riders."

"I had it backward. . . ." Mike muttered.

"What?" I asked.

"The story. I told it backward. The Zephyr and Garth . . . they're really one people, always have been. Until the Draconians came and ripped them apart. That's when they got dumb, confused, foolish. And the people I thought were Draconians—they were their hired troops, the Conflagrons. How did I get it wrong?"

"You didn't get it wrong, Mike. You got it backward!

It probably came that way through Time . . . in the wake of Bayurd," I said.

Mike grabbed the Draconian's shirt. "You committed genocide by separating the Garths and Zephyrs."

"What's genocide?" I asked. I knew it had to be something bad if Troy was involved.

"It's the extermination of a whole race of people. A horrible evil," Mike explained.

Evil—one of the Endless Paths the creature from Out of Time had showed me. Evil was the void that is too well traveled. And Troy the Draconian planned to lead our shining Bayurd along that path.

"You're not getting my Zephyr," I said.

Troy just laughed. "You like playing with fire, Freakface?"

I shoved Troy against the wall. "Try me, nosewipe."

Troy straightened his shirt, smiling as he looked around the room. "This is a chilly place, this town called Ashby. Perhaps I should ask my troops to warm it up around here."

"What?" I gasped, trying to swallow my sudden fear.

The door opened, bringing with it a loud clamor. Kids erupted from their seats like helium balloons.

"Ah!" Troy smiled. "Look who's here."

Santa Claus pushed through the crowd like a conquering hero. But it wasn't Quin under that red suit; he was across the room, still hanging out with my mother.

This Santa was big and round, his head hidden under a floppy red hat. His face was masked by a fluffy beard and round Granny glasses. He looked more real than any Santa I had ever seen. But I knew a Bom when I smelled one.

"No . . ." I gasped.

"Yes!" Troy said. "Aren't we just the jolliest crew you've ever seen? Really getting into the spirit of the holidays!"

"You monster!" Mike said.

"Monster? Not I," Troy said. "But look! Here come Santa's helpers!"

Ten giant elves, clad in green from head to toe, followed after Santa. Their heads were covered with big hats and funny beards. Their huge feet wore giant clown shoes. The elves circled the room, dispensing candy from their sacks and leaking smoke from their beards.

Jumpin' Joe gobbled the candy faster than the kids, singing "Joy to the World" in that ripped-up voice of his. The path called Joy had been a gleaming scarlet ribbon, rippling with starshine and moonkisses.

As I tried to cling to the path called Joy, it dissolved into smoke.

# 27

SANTA CLAUS WAS NAUGHTY INSTEAD
of nice.

The Bom and his LizardPuke elves were holding
the shelter hostage while Mike, Jill, and I took the
Draconian to retrieve Bayurd. No one inside St.
Mark's, including Quin and my mother, had any
idea they were hostages. The Bom had started passing out gifts, and everyone was having a wonderful
time.

"Give me the Zephyr!" Troy shouted.

As Jill led Bayurd out of the shed, he blinked
against the weak afternoon sun. I was ready with a
huge basket of lettuce and other greens. The Zephyr
came straight to me and nibbled the food out of my
hands.

"He's beautiful," breathed Mike.

"He's mine," said the Draconian.

Bayurd startled at Troy's voice. He reared, flashing sharp hooves.

"Whoa! Calm down." Jill grabbed a fistful of mane. The creature's hooves dug at the icy pavement, but as long as Jill held his mane, it seemed he couldn't run, even though he wanted to.

"I'm sorry, fella," I said. "We don't want to give you up. But they'll kill all those kids . . . our families . . ." Bayurd's hide flowed with deep reds and golds. "You know what that's like, don't you?"

He bowed his head.

"Let me have him!" Troy ordered.

"No, wait, he needs to eat," Jill said. "He won't get you far if he's hungry. Nick, give me some more lettuce."

I reached back for the basket. Then I heard it.

*Chomp chomp.*

"Burlap!" I yelled. "You idiot! Get inside!"

"Forget the bum." Troy kicked Burlap aside. "Time to go for a ride." He pulled a harness out of his jacket. The bridle bristled with light, almost as if Troy held pure electricity in his hands.

"Optical fiber," Mike said.

"Pillsbury, you're right again! A smart fellow like you would do well in my Universe. Want a job?" Troy grinned.

"It's amazing," Jill said.

"It's deadly," Mike said. "That's a recirculating

**172**

laser. One false move—"

"And off with his head?" Troy laughed. "The Zephyr is too valuable for that. But if he disobeys, it will not be a pleasant experience, I guarantee you." Troy snapped the harness on the creature's head. Then he pushed Jill aside.

"See you later!" The Draconian grinned and swung onto Bayurd's back.

In a flash, Troy flew through the air. *CLUNK!* He landed on the Dumpster.

"Quick! Run!" I yelled.

"*Th*top!" yelled a giant elf. Green Eyes whipped off his cap and mask.

Mike went white and shaky. "What's this?" he said.

"Meet my friend, the Conflagron," I said, and hawked a load of spit in the creature's face. It sizzled and evaporated.

Green Eyes opened his mouth. A glob of fire percolated in his throat. He was ready to spit it back at me. "What's your problem?" I yelped. "Don't you know a sign of respect when you see one?"

Meanwhile, Jill whipped the laser harness off Bayurd's head. Then she rubbed snow on his scorched face. As Green Eyes kept us cornered, Troy painfully limped back to us.

"You will bend your back to me!" he roared.

The Zephyr turned his head to me, his eyes clearer than spring water. *I bend my back to no one.*

**173**

Jill's eyes met mine. Her fingers loosened on Bayurd's mane. I began to nod—*Yes, let him go.*

"If the beast will not cooperate, then go burn the party guests!" Troy roared.

*"No!"* Mike, Jill, and I shouted together. Jill tightened her grip again.

Troy smiled. "I'm sick of hearing no. When am I going to hear yes?"

Jill's eyes were still locked on mine. "Yes," she whispered. Without turning from me, she offered her other hand to Troy. "He will bend his back to me."

"Wonderful! You're a lovely lass," the Draconian said. "It will be a pleasure having you at my side as I conquer the Universe."

With one hand still clutching the Zephyr's mane, Jill and Troy climbed on his back. The Zephyr quivered with disgust, but he kept his back straight.

Jill gave me a last sad smile, then she turned to Mike. "Tell Mom and Dad . . . I . . . I don't know when I'll be home." Jill pulled sideways on the Zephyr's mane. "Let's go."

"No!" I cried, but before I could call Jill's name, the Zephyr had already disappeared around the back of the church and reappeared in the front.

"They're circling the church," Mike said. "Trying to build up speed to jump out of Time."

Jill guided Bayurd while Troy sat behind her, her knight in shining armor gone very bad. They came around a second time, then a third.

On the fourth circuit, Jill yanked Bayurd to the left, heading him straight for the church's vast stone wall.

"No, Jill, don't!" I yelled.

"We bend our backs to no one!" she shouted. Then Jill flung her hands in the air and let go of the Zephyr.

Bayurd bucked wildly, sending Jill and Troy flying over his head. Jill crashed against the stone wall, crumpling like a flower in the fist of a madman. Flying behind her, Troy hit her instead of the wall. The Zephyr was gone in a flash, even before Jill and Troy hit the ground.

My heart stopped.

Jill was terribly, terribly hurt. She was barely breathing, and her head poured blood.

"Go get my mother!" I cried, and Mike was up, running to the door.

Green Eyes cut Mike down with a blast of fire. And suddenly, fire was everywhere. *There is no place to run,* I thought. *This is the end, and it isn't a blaze of glory.*

It was a blaze of fury.

Then I heard hoofbeats, and in a flash, we leaped across Time once again.

# 28

I HELD JILL IN MY ARMS. HER HEAD oozed blood, her breath came in gulps, her eyes were open but not seeing. Mike was a few feet from me, his skin scorched to a deep red. He cried out in pain, but there was nothing I could do for him.

Jill was dying, and Mike was in agony. Beyond Mike was a crumpled lump—Burlap had gotten swept into the time warp with us again. And again, he was a quivering mess of a man. We were wrapped in a cloud of smoke, and all I could see was dread.

Until something flashed through the smoke. Something silver.

Bayurd had found us. When he saw Jill in my arms, he flew to us. He bent his head low and covered her face with silver tears. He made no sound, but I could hear his wailing in the deepest part of my own heart.

"This is all your fault!" I shrieked at him.

"No, it's not," Jill whispered.

"Jill?" I hoped so hard, it hurt to breathe.

The blood had stopped gushing from her head. Her breathing calmed. The Zephyr's tears that streamed down her face washed away the blood, and, somehow, the hurt and the danger.

Jill's eyes opened slowly. Then she smiled and said, "Not the best rider in the world, am I?"

I smiled back. "Your sense of direction stinks."

"Where's my brother?"

I gently let her go and ran to Mike, who still writhed in torment. I tried to pick him up so I could take him to the Zephyr. His skin was crisp, and he screamed when I touched him.

"He needs help," I cried to the Zephyr. "Please!"

Jill put her arms around Bayurd's neck and he helped her over to where Mike lay. Then she and I steadied Mike as the Zephyr now cried over him. Within seconds, the angry red of Mike's skin faded, and he breathed comfortably.

"The healing touch of a unicorn," Mike said as he sat up. "Thank you." He touched the last tear on Bayurd's face.

"But he's not a unicorn, remember?" I said. "He's a Zephyr."

"Whatever he is, he's wonderful." Jill smiled, stroking the creature's face.

Relief swept over us in waves. Mike and Jill were going to be okay. We had our Zephyr with us. Troy and his nasty friends were nowhere in sight.

It was only when we were wiping away our own tears that we looked around to figure out where we had tumbled to.

It looked like we were in Hell.

Walls of flame stretched to the sky, disappearing into clumps of heavy smoke. We didn't feel the heat because of the rules of the time warp—we weren't really here, not yet. My watch said 5:35 P.M. Assuming the usual rules were in effect, it was probably 12:05 A.M. here. Wherever *here* was.

"Where are we?" Jill's voice shook.

"I'll go look." Mike got up and walked toward the wall of fire.

"Don't," I said. "You'll burn."

"No, I won't," he said. He moved through the flames as if they weren't there.

"Why can we walk through the fire?" I asked as we followed him. "We can't walk through doors and walls."

"I've given a lot of thought to your time warp," Mike answered. "If things are fixed, like buildings and trees, then you can't pass through them because they exist in that place, in long stretches of time. But things that move, like people and fire, things that exist in space for that moment of time but may move in the next moment—those you can move right through."

"And we don't feel anything because we're not really here," Jill said.

"Not yet," I added. I checked my watch again. When we actually got here in seven hours, I didn't want to be here. I wanted to get to someplace where there was no fire.

But as we walked through the sheets of flame, we realized that might not be such a simple thing to do. We walked and walked, but we couldn't find anything we could identify as buildings or trees or fences. Just hot, hot fire.

"Oh heck," I said. "We forgot something."

"What?" Mike asked. "We've got the Zephyr!" The creature followed wherever Jill led.

Jill and I looked at each other. "Burlap," we said together.

We had no landmarks to guide our way back. Every lick of flame looked the same. Jill finally called out, "What a nice salad. All that lettuce and spinach and . . ."

We waited a minute, then heard a familiar *pum-pum-pum*. Burlap stumbled out of the flames, looking as confused as ever.

"Stay with us! We have to stick together!" I scolded him.

"But where are we?" Jill asked.

**179**

Mike shrugged. "We could be on another planet, even. After all, your Zephyr made it to Earth on his own. Since he can cut through Time and Space, there's no holding him to any *where* or any *time*."

"Not true!" I said. "There is something holding him to Earth. Otherwise, he would have left long ago."

"Tell me this isn't Earth," Jill gasped. "Please."

I tripped, then fell face first on a granite step. I wiped away layers of soot and read "Ashby, Incorporated 1826."

It was the first step that led up to Ashby Town Hall. "Oh no," I said. "Please, don't let this be."

Mike gasped. Jill buried her face in the Zephyr's mane. Burlap stood behind us, unmoving and apparently unmoved.

After a few minutes of pained silence, Mike said, "Come on. We'd better see how far the fire goes."

We walked through another wall of flames to find scorched buildings, charred trees, and melted cars. Ashby Common looked like a giant ashtray.

Jill stroked Bayurd's face. "Can't you heal this, too?"

But all the tears of all the Zephyrs in all the worlds couldn't put this fire out.

We walked from one corner of Ashby to the other. Burlap followed like a confused mutt, Bayurd like a scared puppy. It was the same wherever we went—

**180**

burning buildings, most still with flames exploding from their walls and roofs. Trees, bushes, fences, trucks, cars—everything was ash or on its way there.

Ashby Middle School was gone, along with the high school, the library, the town hall. Our neighborhood was in flames.

Jill lay facedown in the fire and cried.

Mike threw himself against the wall of his half-burned house. "Mom! Dad!" he wailed. I finally pulled Mike away before he broke every bone in his body.

"There's nothing we can do!" I shouted.

Mike pounded the crap out of me, and I let him. Finally, he collapsed next to Jill.

"Where did it start?" Jill moaned.

"You know where," I said. "And you know when."

"St. Mark's," Mike said, his voice ripped apart from crying.

We wandered back that way, not knowing what else to do. The mall and hospital were completely gone. The walls of flame grew higher as we approached St. Mark's. Through the sheets of yellow-white, we could see stone rubble that was once the church.

"Mom . . . the kids . . ." I mumbled. Jill hugged me for all she was worth.

"We have to do something," I said.

"How can we?" Jill cried. "There's nothing we can

do in these time warps until time catches up. And once time does that, it's too late."

"Then we have to start walking away from this fire to save ourselves," I said.

"Why bother . . ." Jill whispered.

"Maybe there's no use anyway. Maybe the whole world is on fire," Mike said.

"No!" I shouted. "No one should die!"

"We can't stop it!" Mike sobbed. "It's already happened!"

Something itched in my mind, nibbling through all my pain and fear. "It's happening now . . . but *we* haven't happened yet."

"Stop it!" Jill said. "All that stupid fantasy talk did this to us! Stop it!"

"No, let me think this out. When we left, this wasn't happening yet. Or maybe it was just beginning to happen."

"But we're here," Mike said. "And we're powerless until *now* resumes. And when we get back to *now*, this will have already happened! Once we get back in Time, we will be out of time."

"So we have to go back and stop it," I said.

"How can we do that?" Mike asked. "Time only goes forward."

*Sometimes the best step forward is one step backward.*

I looked up at Bayurd. "But we have a friend who can cut through Space and Time. A friend who

**182**

wanders Out of Time, looking for . . ."

"Looking for his rider! Maybe if he has his rider, he'll be able to control his time traveling!" Jill said.

"He let you ride him," I reminded her. "Maybe you're the one he's looking for."

"He tolerated me," she said. "But I'm not his True Rider."

"His True Rider? What is that?" Mike asked.

Jill looked at Bayurd, her eyes clearing through the haze of grief. "That's who he's been looking for all this time. Someone brave and loyal and . . ."

"And nuts?" I yelped.

Mike stared at me. "Ever ride a horse?" he asked.

# 29

JiLL STEADiED BAYURD WHiLE i approached him. What was the worst that could happen? Even if he tossed me to the ground and trampled me, it couldn't be any worse than seeing my town and—my heart stopped again—my family and friends go up in flames.

"Okay, buddy," I whispered. "Please bend your back to me." I climbed up, seeing the world from on high. It was still Hell.

The Zephyr's mane tingled in my hand. Something tingled in my brain but I couldn't find the thought, not with all the fear cruising through my body.

"Let him go," I said to Jill, who clutched Bayurd's mane.

"In a minute," she said. She motioned me to bend

down. I leaned over, my face near hers.

She kissed me.

It felt so good, I couldn't breathe.

"Ride well, Freakface," she said. Then she let go of the Zephyr's mane.

Bayurd bucked hard. My stomach lurched through the air, with the rest of my body barely attached. I hit the ground with a hard *whap*.

Bayurd looked at me, his eyes shining with apologies. *I cannot bend my back to you.*

"Not me," I said, spitting out the very tip of my tongue. I had bitten it off on the way down.

"I didn't think it would be you," Mike said. "I must be the True Rider. I'm the one who knows aliens, who dreams big dreams . . ."

"You're the one who got us into all this trouble. So get up here," Jill said. She stroked Bayurd while Mike, pale-faced and clammy, climbed onto the Zephyr's back.

"Did I ever tell you I get motion sickness?" he whimpered.

"Oh, so it's barf I smell and not your cheap cologne," I joked.

"Just shut up and ride!" Jill said, then let go.

Mike flew up like a missile and down like a rock. He almost brained Burlap. "We're doomed," Mike moaned.

"We can't be!" Jill yelled. "I refuse to be doomed!"

"This is useless. He won't let any of us ride him!"

**185**

Mike yelled back.

That tingling grew stronger in my head. "Not all of us have tried yet," I said, looking at Burlap. Burlap crowded deeper into his rags, hiding his face.

"Nick, he's not Cinderella," Mike snapped.

"He has to try," I said. "He's the only person left."

"Are you nuts?" Jill shrieked. "How is he supposed to help us when he can't even help himself? Look at him! He's a lost soul."

I looked at Burlap. He seemed scrawnier than ever, shrunken inside his wrappings, his eyes cloudy, his face shaggy with beard and burlap wrappings.

Then I looked at Mike. He stared at Burlap in a terrible and true way. Judging him. "And why is he so lost?" Mike asked.

"You know what the homeless have to deal with," Jill said. "Alcoholism, unemployment, abuse—"

"Mental or physical illness, bad luck," I said, sounding like Quin. "Or . . ." Light began to dawn for me, too.

"Or what?" Jill demanded.

"Or maybe he's homeless because someone burned him out of his home," I said.

"And maybe he's confused because he's not used to being alone!" Mike added.

"Maybe he just needs someone to help him get moving!" I cheered.

"Maybe he just needs us to give him a hand up!" Mike added.

I grabbed Burlap's arm. "Get up!" I hollered.

Burlap didn't move.

Mike grabbed his other arm. "I don't know, Nick. He's pretty scrawny."

"This is nuts," Jill said. "You can't put this poor guy on Bayurd. He'll get killed!"

"He's our last hope," I said.

Mike and I shoved Burlap toward the Zephyr. The guy shook inside his rags, terrified. I grabbed his face, trying to make his eyes lock onto mine. "I need you to b-believe . . ." I stuttered. What? What did I need him to believe? "I need you to believe in yourself."

Burlap's eyes caught mine. They cleared, only for an instant.

"Come on, pal," I said. "Up and over."

Mike and I lifted him onto the Zephyr's back, then held our breaths. He sat there like a stupid stone.

"Jill, let go," I whispered.

"You know what I believe? I believe this is cruel. I believe this is stupid," Jill whispered. "I believe this poor guy is going to get killed."

"I believe everyone has something great in him," I shouted. "So let go!"

Jill slipped her hands out of the Zephyr's mane.

The Zephyr reared, his hooves flashing silver. I closed my eyes and waited for the *thud* that meant Burlap had been thrown halfway across the world.

It never came.

Silver light flooded us, so bright that it shone through my closed eyes.

"Look!" Jill cried, her voice soaring.

Burlap sat astride Bayurd. His rags had somehow transformed into a glowing tunic, his shaggy hair into long curls, his huddled form now straight and proud. His eyes were clear, like endless streams of water.

Burlap had become a shining knight, far beyond our wildest dreams.

He looked through me and knew me. "Friend," he and Bayurd said together, not in a voice, but in a tone that we clearly understood. "Thank you."

Then they rode out of sight and Out of Time.

Jill, Mike, and I had decided to stay in Ashby for the end of our world.

"I can't leave Mom and Dad . . ." Jill sobbed.

I had no tears left. We had restored Bayurd and his true Garth and they had left us. The final betrayal.

Time ticked on my wrist. Now 11:48 P.M.

*Should I tell Jill I love her before we die?*

11:49 P.M.

*Should I tell Mike I forgive him for bringing aliens to Earth? And that he will be my best friend forever, even if forever only lasts another fifteen minutes?*

11:50 P.M.

*Should I scream for help? Why bother? There's never a loyal Sirian around when you need one. Or a cop. Or a teacher. Or a shelter director.*

11:51 P.M.

*Or a father.*

11:52 P.M.

"Nick?" Mike said.

"Um." I couldn't even form words anymore.

"Do you hear it?"

"What?" I said. That one word almost killed me.

"The music of the stars," Mike said in a breath. "Hear it? The low tones . . ."

"I hear something," Jill said, lifting her face out of her hands.

"There's a rhythm to it," Mike said, almost smiling. "Kind of peaceful . . ."

"That's not music!" I shouted. "That's hoofbeats!"

# 30

AN ARMY OF LIGHT THUNDERED THROUGH the flames.

Burlap and Bayurd led a legion of Zephyrs and Garths into the fire. Bayurd was the only creature with a horn, but the others were just as fast and sleek, and their riders were just as tall and proud as the guy formerly known as Burlap.

"Reynald," Jill said. "That's his real name. Except . . ."

"They aren't separate individuals," Mike said. "The horse and rider form one person."

Reynald and Bayurd bowed low to us. "I am sorry for running off," they said as one voice. "But I needed help. Now, if you could show me the way back . . ."

"The way back?" I yelped. "Don't you know the way?"

"It is your path," Reynald-Bayurd said. "You need to show me the first step."

*Sometimes the best step forward is one step backward.*

But which way was back? When I was in that world that was Out of Time, the Endless Paths stretched in countless directions. Which should we choose to ride back on?

Despair, maybe. Mike, Jill, and I had been soaking in it.

Or perhaps hate. I despised the Draconian and his LizardPukes. They had no regard for any people, be they human or Zephyr-Garth. I remembered the path of hate now, another well-traveled road of changing colors. Once you got on that road, it was almost impossible to get off.

Jill grabbed my wrist. "Nick, there's only two minutes left." My watch read 12:03 A.M. "We have to get back before the Conflagrons start spitting fire all over town."

"Which way, Nick?" Mike squealed.

"How would I know?" I yelped.

"Because you are the one who found me when I was wandering," Reynald-Bayurd said. "You know the way."

"We're almost out of time!" Jill cried.

Out of Time. *The Ways are Endless.* But we needed the way back to the moment before the fire started. Maybe courage? I closed my eyes and saw it:

a narrow path of deep gray, determined, strong. Not a place I was used to treading.

Love, perhaps? A glittering path that was almost impossible to follow and yet woven through all the other paths in a design that held them all together.

"Nick, hurry!" Jill squeezed my hand. Her hand tingled in mine. Like the Zephyr's mane. Like the friendship that had bound me and Mike for all these years. Like the golden cord . . . the one that Reynald, as Burlap, had lost in his own pocket.

It suddenly made sense—that's what the scumbag Troy had been searching the shelter for. He knew that Burlap was the other half of the Zephyr. Burlap was useless to the Draconian because Troy wanted to take his place and ride the Zephyr himself. But Troy knew the cord would help him find his way—the cord that was still in my jeans pocket.

I pulled it out and handed it to Reynald-Bayurd. It was suddenly quite clear which way we needed to go. "Hope," I said. "That's where we'll go."

Reynald-Bayurd snapped the cord over our heads. It opened like a ribbon, then opened again like a broad road, then magnified a third time into a flowing river of gold.

Reynald-Bayurd jumped in and we all followed.

The Bom and his LizardPuke elves were holding the shelter hostage while Mike, Jill, and I took the Draconian to retrieve Bayurd. No one inside St.

**192**

Mark's, including Quin and my mother, had any idea they were hostages. The Bom had started passing out gifts, and everyone was having a wonderful time.

"Give me the Zephyr!" Troy shouted.

Jill, Mike, and I fell on each other, blubbering like babies.

"We're not too late," Jill whispered. "We're back where we started!"

"Things have changed," Mike said. "Tell him, Nick."

"We're running a sale today," I said with a grin. "A hundred Zephyrs for the price of one." Reynald-Bayurd stormed from the back alley, leading his army of knights.

Troy's eyes bugged out of his head. "What are they doing here? I thought we—"

"Ripped us all apart?" Reynald-Bayurd asked, his voice ringing inside our heads. "Yes, you ripped my family apart on Grayle. But we're an ancient race, living across the stars. My cousins have gathered from every corner of the galaxy to fight your evil scheme."

"As long as my troops hold the Earth brats, you won't dare harm me. And if you go in and fight them at that pathetic Christmas party, you will expose this planet to neutralization. So we are at an impasse," Troy snarled.

"The creep is right," Mike said. "We can't go

charging in there and fight the Conflagrons. Even if the kids didn't get hurt, everyone would see what was happening. There are reporters in there, even. We can't reveal the aliens to them!"

"So, now what?" Jill asked.

"Give me what I want," said Troy. "I'll leave peacefully."

"You're not taking the Zephyr!" I yelled.

"A consolation prize, then." Troy smiled.

"Forget it! I'm not going with you!" Jill stormed.

Troy's mouth twisted in a sarcastic sneer. "What would I want you for? If I can't have the Zephyr, at least let me take the only other thing of value on this backward planet."

"What's that?" I asked.

Troy pointed at Mike. "The Pillsbury. He's scrawny, weak, whiny. But he's got a clear head on his shoulders. Make a good executive assistant."

"No!" Jill yelled.

Mike puffed with pride, then paled with fear. "Maybe I should go," he said. "If it's the only way to get him and his flamethrowers off the planet."

"Don't take away my best friend!" I wailed loudly, grabbing Mike. "Pretend you're going with him," I whispered between my annoying sobs. "I need a diversion."

Mike pulled away from me, wiping away the spit he had sneaked onto his face to fake tears. "Okay, Draconian. I'll go with you," he said. "But first we

**194**

have to negotiate my salary."

"No!" Reynald-Bayurd cried.

"You're not leaving this planet!" Jill whacked Mike. "I'm not done with you, Geekface."

*Trust me,* I thought deep inside my head. Both Reynald-Bayurd and Jill looked at me. Startled.

Then they nodded.

While Mike was bargaining for vacation time on some planet named Sunstroke, I slipped inside to the party.

It was the happiest occasion I had ever seen.

The Bom, dressed as Santa Claus, had passed out the presents. The kids were surrounded by wrapping paper and dolls and trucks and new sweaters. The ten LizardPukes, still disguised as giant elves, guarded every door. Quin and Mom stood in the corner, drinking hot chocolate.

Quin grabbed me in a bear hug. "Having a good time?"

"Quin," I said, "you said once that next time a situation came up, I should come to you."

Quin's smile faded. "Of course."

"Well, a situation has come up."

"What? What can I do to help?" Quin asked.

"Just trust me," I said softly. "Please. Even if I start acting weirder than usual." I stared at Quin.

"Are you in some sort of trouble? Maybe I should—"

"You shouldn't do anything," I said. "I have to handle this."

"This? *This* what?"

"Please, Quin. Don't sell me short. Trust me on this. No questions asked."

Quin stared for a long moment. "Okay. No questions asked."

I walked through the room, finally recognizing Green Eyes through his elf mask. In a few minutes, he would come out and spit fire on Mike Pillsbury— the first flicker on the road to Hell. We had to change that.

"So many losers, so little time," I said loudly. Heads turned to me, faces puzzled.

"Hey there." I punched Green Eyes's chest. "What freak show did you fall out of?"

Smoke drifted out of the top of his elf hat.

"Do you need a license to be that ugly?" I continued.

Behind me rose a sound like a strangled whale. One of the elves—I'd have bet anything it was Crusty—was laughing.

I walked over to him. "Hey, it's my old pal. What're you doing here? Did someone dig up a septic tank?"

Mom, frowning, started toward me. Quin held her back.

Crusty shifted nervously.

"Next time you climb out of the slime, try brushing your teeth. Your breath smells like something

**196**

that comes out of the back end of my dog."

Crusty moved on me. The Bom—still incognito as the world's slimiest Santa Claus—stepped in between us.

"Hey, Santa Claus! How can you tell if a Bom is lying?"

"Shut up, Freakface," the Bom hissed.

"His lips are moving!" I shouted.

Santa motioned to his elves. The LizardPukes surrounded me. Quin moved toward the circle, but I waved him back.

"Hey Santa, what's the difference between a dead Bom and a dead snake on the road?"

The Bom's fake white beard rippled as angry gas bubbles erupted from Santa's suit.

"There's skid marks in front of the snake! Get it? Skid marks!" I laughed in Santa's face. "No one is going to bother to slow down for a slime-sucking, gas-blowing lawyer. I mean Bom."

"Get him!" the Bom yelled.

Bingo.

The LizardPukes advanced on me. I backed toward the door. "Come on, you fakers," I said. "I'm not afraid of any booger-nosed, buck-toothed elves. Come on."

Mom tried to step between me and the army of elves. "Nick, you're being rude! What are you doing?"

Quin's eyes met mine. *Don't sell me short,* I mouthed.

Quin pulled Mom back. "No questions asked," he said sternly.

I waved as I booked it out the side door, followed by a horde of steaming elves.

Quin was a good man to have on your side in a situation. Even when he didn't have a clue.

# 31

IT WAS OVER QUICKER THAN YOU CAN say "Boms stink."

I leaped into the side alley with the LizardPukes hot on my tail. They erupted with a fireball bigger than the Dumpster. My heart stopped. *It's going to happen after all,* I thought. *All this, and we still bring Hell to Ashby.*

Then Reynald-Bayurd dipped his horn into the flames. The firestorm disappeared.

"Up there!" Jill shouted.

Like a comet blazing across the sky, Reynald-Bayurd had rerouted the fireball into the air. It flamed for a few short seconds, then was swallowed up by the night.

"Fire again!" Troy yelled.

While the LizardPukes were recharging their

flammable drool, the army of Zephyr-Garths charged. They swept up the Conflagrons, binding them before they could even spit a single spark.

That left Troy and his slimy attorney still standing.

"We'll sue!" the Bom said, ripping off his Santa suit. "We have a court order!"

"You *had* a court order!" a voice squeaked.

Titan peeked out from behind the Dumpster. "The Federation court has issued a restraining order against the Draconians. In light of new evidence uncovered on Grayle."

"What new evidence?" Troy squealed. "We destroyed every—*oof*." The Bom slapped him with a tentacle to shut him up.

"While I was dealing with issues here on Earth, my colleagues reopened the investigation on Grayle. At our own expense, I might add." Titan sniffed at me. "Barnabus and Ditka found enough irregularities to persuade the court to reverse its decision."

"And now we're going to nail you." Mike waved a tiny cassette under the Draconian's nose. "A Christmas present. A micro-videocam. I used it to tape our whole encounter . . . including your account of what really happened on Grayle."

"Come along, Draconian," said Titan. "The Judge is expecting you. And bring your slippery attorney with you. You'll need him."

Reynald-Bayurd bound Troy in an iron-gray cord, then motioned to his army. They herded their

Conflagron prisoners and followed Titan to the back parking lot.

"Hey! Sirian!" I shouted.

Titan turned. "Yes, Freakface?"

"Sorry I called you a rat."

"Well, yes. Sorry I called you . . . foolish."

"Hey, if that's the worst thing anyone calls me, it's a good day." I laughed.

The Bom followed the procession like a washed-out worm, his tentacles dragging.

"Ho-ho-ho," I snorted as he walked by.

He stopped and turned to me. "Freakface, here's my card, if you decide to sue. The Conflagrons don't have a cent, but the Draconians have deep pockets."

"Hey, Bom. What's the difference between a leech and a Bom?" I asked.

"What?" the Bom said.

"When you die, a leech stops sucking your blood and drops off." I ripped up the Bom's card. "Get off my planet."

"You'll be sorry, Freakface. I could make you rich beyond your wildest dreams."

"I already am, Stinkface," I said.


Jill stroked Reynald-Bayurd's side. "I'm going to miss you," she said.

"I will miss you, too," he said. "But I've been stumbling around for too long. First we have to find the survivors on Grayle and help reunite them. And then we've got work to do. The Sirians are involved in some desperate situations, and my people can help."

"Before you go," Mike said, "I have a question."

"Yes?"

"Why didn't you recognize each other? I mean, yourself?" Mike asked. "You two were together a lot when the Zephyr part of you was cruising with Nick and Jill, and the Burlap part was hanging out at the shelter and around town. Why didn't you know it was yourself?"

"The hardest thing to do in any world is to find yourself," Reynald-Bayurd said. "And as long as I was separated, I didn't know what I was missing. I only knew I was hungry . . ."

"No kidding!" Jill laughed.

"And lonely. It's terrible to have part of yourself ripped away." Reynald-Bayurd dipped his horn to me. "Isn't it?"

I nodded. I didn't dare talk; I'd leak out tears.

"Thank you, Jill. Thank you, Mike. And thank you, Nick."

I hugged the Zephyr part, then I hugged the Garth part. "Next time a situation comes up, you come to us," I whispered.

Reynald-Bayurd smiled. A silver hush fell over us. The icy December evening was suddenly warm. From inside the shelter, we could hear kids' laughter and Christmas carols.

"Time to go," Titan said.

Reynald-Bayurd dipped his horn. A bumpy brown path opened up. "Justice," Titan said. "It's a rocky road, but well worth the trip." Reynald-Bayurd stepped on, followed by Titan, then the army of Zephyr-Garths and their smoldering prisoners.

The hoofbeats lingered long after the road disappeared. Then I was alone in the alley with Mike, Jill, and the Dumpster.

"So, Mike. You got that micro-videocam for Christmas," I said. "Except Christmas hasn't come yet."

"Oh, well. Maybe I was a little naughty." Mike grinned. "What about you, Nick? What are you getting for Christmas?"

I hooked one arm around him and the other around Jill. "I'll settle for peace on Earth and goodwill to people, thank you."


Quin wanted to take me and Mom out for a late supper. "I love the shelter," he said with a sigh. "But even I get sick of the food after a while."

We planned to stop at our old house so I could get washed up. "You stink!" Mom said. "If I find you've been smoking . . ."

"No way!" I swore. "That side alley by the shelter gets pretty nasty sometimes. Right, Quin?"

Quin's eyes sparkled. "Right."

As we drove through Ashby Center, I went kind

**203**

of nuts. "Hello, Town Hall! Hello, Library!" I yelled. "Hey, look, there's the drugstore. And the police station! And the stone wall on the Common!"

Mom felt my forehead. "Are you okay, Nick? You sound rather delirious."

"He's okay, Allie," Quin said. "Just got a touch of the holiday happies, that's all."

We pulled into the driveway and found our garage under construction.

"Wh-a-a-t?" Mom stuttered. "We just left six hours ago and . . ."

The new structure was crawling with workmen. Dana Pillsbury fluttered around, supervising.

"They showed up two hours ago." Dana beamed. "Said they were hired by someone who just wanted to do a good deed for the holidays. You've never seen workers like these fellows."

No, indeed. A painter had a tentacle hanging out of his shirt. A carpenter kept forgetting himself and floating off his ladder. A plumber worked with a German shepherd constantly at his side—a dog that wore a collar with a little box attached.

"They're real go-getters," Dana went on. "Pam has already tried to hire them to build an exercise room for us, but they said they have another job really far away. Imagine, rebuilding this garage in one afternoon? These guys are out of this world."

The new garage had been doubled in size to house both our junk, the Looses' junk, and a couple of cars. Above the garage were two more stories—Mom and I would have big bedrooms and our own bathrooms, as well as plenty of room for entertaining friends.

The way Mom and Quin were holding hands, I suspected we'd need that extra room.

"This is pretty darn awesome," Mom said, her smile bigger than it had been for a long, long time.

"This is pretty darn suspicious," Quin whispered in my ear. Then he grinned. "But no questions asked, right?"

"Right," I said.

When we came back from supper, Quin played Scrabble with us in our new family room. The workers had moved in new furniture and a wide-screen television set. They even had decorated a Christmas tree for us before they left.

Someone had nibbled the bottom branches, but we didn't care. In fact, I kind of liked it that way.

# 32

i ALMOST GOT LOST iN MY NEW
bedroom.

It was a palace. My bathroom was bigger than
my old bedroom, complete with Jacuzzi and shower.
My walk-in closet was as big as my half sisters' bedroom. My room had built-in shelves for my new
computer, television, and VCR.

A note had been left on my pillow. "We hope this
will compensate in a small way for the damage done
by the Draconians and Conflagrons. Sincerely, Titan."

In a small way? I flopped onto my new water bed
and floated in luxury.

But when I got ready for bed, my cartoon pajamas
were missing. Sure, I had new football pajamas, a
flannel bathrobe, and leather slippers. I had a whole
new wardrobe, complete with the latest sports

jacket and hat. But I missed my ratty old baseball cap. I missed my favorite socks that had no toes left. I had awesome posters on my walls, but I missed my old pictures of Mike and me going to kindergarten with big smiles and no front teeth.

I had gained. But I had lost, too.

As I was turning out my lights—with a remote control—I heard a familiar *pum-pum* that grew into a *pound-pound*.

Before I could say "Welcome back!" I was Out of Time.

"This is a rare privilege," Reynald-Bayurd said. "Very few In-Spacers get to come here, and you've been here twice."

The Endless Ways stretched around us—tones and colors and emotions and truths going every way, but always onward.

"Why am I here?" I asked.

"The Galactic Federation has tried to compensate you for your efforts and losses," Reynald-Bayurd explained. "But certain folks realize that, if part of me had fallen into the hands of the Draconians, the very fabric of the Universe could have been threatened. And for that, I have been given permission to assist you in whatever desire you have."

"I don't understand," I muttered, almost hypnotized by the possibilities as they flowed by.

"What do you want most in the world? Or out of the world?" Reynald-Bayurd asked. "I've been given permission to give it to you."

The same offer that the Bom had made! But this one came with no strings attached. I had refused the Bom for two reasons: I wouldn't give up the Zephyr, no matter what; and the Bom couldn't give me what I really wanted anyway.

The Bom couldn't turn back the hands of Time.

But Reynald-Bayurd could.

We had used his power to go back in Time and stop a burning Hell that threatened to destroy my whole town. Why not step a little farther back in Time and stop that burning anger that had destroyed my family?

The path under my feet glowed like honey. Hope, I knew. It washed through me like a summer shower, bringing the smell of sunshine.

Reynald-Bayurd could step me back five, maybe six years. Maybe I could go back to that time Mom and Dad argued over the new carpet; Mom thought we couldn't afford it, but Dad thought we needed to cover the whole house in it.

"The bottom line, Alice, is that you never have any fun."

"The bottom line, Don, is that you have too much fun."

Mom had to work weekends for two months to pay for the new carpeting. Knowing what I know

**208**

now, I might have the right words to stop my parents' ugly words.

But that was only one of the many fights my parents had had. I had to choose carefully. The different arguments ricocheted around in my head like it was yesterday. And it could be; it could be now, if I were to just give Reynald-Bayurd the word.

Should I?

But if somehow I turned the tide of my parents' marriage and got back what I had lost, then would I lose something else?

I wished Mike were here. Or Jill.

"Nick?" Reynald-Bayurd said softly.

"I know, we don't have all day."

"Actually, we do. Is there something I can do to help you make your decision?"

*Sure,* I thought. *Show me all the yesterdays and all the tomorrows and let me pick the ones I like best.* But somehow I knew that even Out of Time couldn't be that sloppy.

"Before I decide, I need to see my father," I said. "Can you take me to Arizona without anyone noticing?"

"If you'll start me on the right path," Reynald-Bayurd said.

The right path? I had to get us there? "How? I don't understand."

*"You don't need to understand,"* a voice said with no body but all being. *"You just need to believe."*

**209**

I watched the silver path of love flow before me. I thought of my dad and the way he threw a base-ball, sidearm with a lefty curve. How he loved lots of sugar on his high-fiber cereal. How he sang in the shower and danced when he washed dishes. How he bought a snowblower, then refused to use it because he needed the exercise he got shoveling.

The silver path turned dusty and broad. A warm breeze swept along it; when I saw the first cactus, I nodded to Reynald-Bayurd. He bent his back to me, and I climbed on behind my friend.

We stepped Out of Time and into Arizona.

Christmas Eve was cloudless and warm, though I couldn't feel the temperature. Reynald-Bayurd had set us fifteen minutes in the future, to give me time to check things out without interference.

The garage door to my father's house was open, allowing me to slip inside. Things were how I had remembered them. I recognized my father's favorite things—the grandfather clock he inherited from his uncle John, the stuffed bass he caught when he was my age, the endless rows of books on history and politics. The one thing I had forgotten was how I hated seeing things from my home, now in someone else's home.

Beverly was asleep in the master bedroom, the baby monitor by her head. Dad wasn't in there.

The door to the nursery was cracked open. I had

to make myself even skinnier than Mike, but I managed to slip inside.

Two-year-old Sara and Tara were still in cribs. I remembered my dad was having money problems. They probably couldn't afford beds. I leaned over Sara's crib—I only knew it was her because of the quilt hanging on the wall that said her name. When I had seen her a year and a half ago, she looked like a blob of baby puke and diaper rash. But now she looked like a person.

She looked like me.

I stepped across to Tara's crib. Same person sleeping there, only in a yellow nightgown instead of green.

She looked like me, too.

It had never occurred to me that they had any part of me in them. My father had left and married a stranger, and together they made strangers.

Who turned out not to be so strange after all.

I looked around the room. Dolls were neatly lined on shelves. But on the floor was the mess of toys they actually played with: trucks and blocks and funny-faced puppets.

The girls liked the same kind of toys I had liked when I was little.

Reynald-Bayurd stuck his horn into the door. "A few more minutes, Nick."

Funny, I didn't pass through either Sara or Tara when I kissed each one on the cheek. No doubt some

**211**

time warp oddity Mike could explain later.

Dad was in his workshop looking at a photo album. My baby pictures.

He had tears in his eyes.

"It's okay, Dad," I whispered. "Some things can be bent and stretched but never broken."

"Nick?" Reynald-Bayurd asked. "Have you decided what you want?"

"Thanks," I said. "But I already have what I want. Let's go home."

When I kissed Dad good-bye, I didn't pass through his face either.

# 33

BiG SURPRiSE. MiKE PiLLSBURY GOT
a micro-videocam for Christmas.

Jill got a new boyfriend, some doofus basketball
player named Clayton. He annoyed the crap out of
me but hey, no one's perfect.

I got a trip to Arizona. Pam Pillsbury nagged the
airline into letting me use her frequent flier miles to
get me to my father. I spent a whole week teaching
my sisters how to flush the toilet and shout "I did
my duty!"

Mom and I spent New Year's Day at St. Mark's.
Jumpin' Joe had just gotten a job grooming dogs,
and we celebrated with ginger ale, pizza, and
brownies.

When we returned to school after the holidays,
Aaron Fleming was grinning like a beauty pageant

host. The dweeb had gotten his two front teeth for Christmas.

I should have kept my mouth shut.

But Fleming couldn't keep his mouth shut. All day he flashed those new pearly whites like he was a toothpaste ad.

"Hey, Fleming, shut your mouth! You're blinding me!" I yelled in the cafeteria. "What beaver did you steal those teeth from? Good grief, you can see them from outer space, they're so big." The whole lunch room laughed, and I laughed with them.

I was still laughing when Fleming tried to knock me into tomorrow.

But I stayed right where I was. Well, actually, I ended up on my butt.

Hey—no one's perfect.